I0546616

Not This Christmas

MADDIE JAMES

SAND DUNE BOOKS

Not This Christmas

Maddie James

A Falls Mountain Romance
Book 5

Copyright © 2018 Maddie James

Not This Christmas

2nd Edition with Extensive Revisions, 2025

Creative Content by Jacobs Ink, LLC

All rights reserved. The unauthorized reproduction or distribution of this copyrighted work, in whole or part, by any electronic, mechanical, or other means, is illegal and forbidden.

This is a work of fiction. Characters, settings, names, and occurrences are a product of the author's imagination and bear no resemblance to any actual person, living or dead, places or settings, and/or occurrences. Any incidences of resemblance are purely coincidental.

This edition is published by Sand Dune Books, Turquoise Morning, LLC dba Jacobs Ink, LLC, PO Box 20, New Holland, OH 43145.

About Falls Mountain

Welcome to Harbor Falls—**where second chances bloom, hearts heal, and love finds its way home in the Blue Ridge Mountains.**

The *Falls Mountain Romance* series delivers heartfelt, semi-sweet love stories filled with small-town charm, found family, and the promise of new beginnings. Each book can be read as a standalone story, but together they celebrate the beauty of hope, healing, and happily ever after.

But on Falls Mountain, love has a habit of showing up unannounced.

From second chances to secret babies to grumpy-sunshine pairings, each book brings a satisfying happily-ever-after and a cast of characters you'll want to visit again and again.

Falls Mountain Romance is a companion series to the Sweet Hart Inn Romance books by Maddie James.

Not This Christmas

A Falls Mountain Romance, Book 5

A heartwarming, faith-filled holiday romance from the Falls Mountain Romance series.

When Nora Patterson rear-ends Reverend Rock Peters' SUV on a snowy mountain road, her Christmas Eve takes an unexpected turn—from lonely to life-changing. Stranded together in an old cabin while a blizzard rages outside, Nora discovers the handsome minister is kind, steady, and far too easy to talk to. She's spent the year missing her mother and praying for someone to share Christmas with—never imagining that the answer to her prayers might come that night.

Rockford Peters made peace long ago with spending his holidays alone, serving others while quietly yearning for someone to come home to. Then Nora literally crashes into his life, bringing warmth and laughter into a heart he thought had stopped hoping.

But when the snow clears, will love stay—or melt away with the morning light?

Snowbound by fate and guided by faith, can two strangers find comfort, courage, and perhaps a Christmas miracle that neither saw coming?

Why You'll Love It

- Snowed-in small-town romance
- Faith, grace, and second chances
- Cozy cabin + Christmas morning magic
- Heartwarming Harbor Falls community cameos
- Perfect for fans of *Falling for Grace* and *The Christmas Nanny*

Not This Christmas is a heartwarming small-town Christmas romance from the Falls Mountain Romance series.

Chapter One

"I really hate to say this," Suzie Hart announced, drawing back a drapery panel and peering out her living room window. "Because I'm having so much fun and I don't want anyone to leave, but if you have to drive anywhere other than Harbor Falls, you might think about leaving soon."

The crowd in Suzie's living room twittered and chattered about.

"Ah, Suzie. It's just a little snow squall," Jack Ackerman explained. "It will be here and gone. Nothing to worry about."

His wife, Jasmine, stepped closer to the window and stood beside Suzie. "I don't know, Jack. Take a look." The two women stared out the window. "Living in Atlanta for so long, I'd forgotten what snow can be like in the mountains," she added. "Should we leave?"

Jack shrugged. "We have four-wheel drive. We'll be fine."

"Is it getting bad out there, girls?" Sydney Hart stepped into the group. "I haven't paid attention to the weather."

Nora Patterson hadn't either. She glanced over at the crowd in Suzie's living room. Some of them appeared to be a tad anxious. "I'm going to Dad's farm this evening. Maybe I should think about heading out."

"All the way to Dalton Springs?" Jack turned and met her gaze. "You have to drive over there tonight?"

"It's Christmas Eve. I don't want Dad to be alone."

He nodded. "Right."

Nora lingered near the dessert table, pretending to study the trays of cookies when in truth she was simply avoiding the couples scattered through Suzie's twinkle-lit living room. Laughter bubbled from the corner, to where Jack and Jasmine had migrated, and were teasing Brad about his ugly Christmas sweater. She smiled—genuinely—but something tugged deep in her chest.

Suzie swept over with her trademark hostess energy, balancing a mug of spiced cider. "You're awfully quiet over here. You doing okay?"

Nora offered a small smile. "Fine. Just admiring the peppermint bark. You really outdid yourself this year."

Suzie nudged her. "That's not what I asked."

Caught, Nora sighed and took the mug. "It's silly, I know. Everyone looks so happy tonight, and I am too, really. It's just... Mom always loved Christmas Eve. This is the first one without her. The house feels different now—quiet." She laughed softly. "Even the cat seems to notice."

Suzie's expression softened. "Grief does that. The quiet gets louder."

"Yeah," Nora murmured, eyes flicking toward the frosted windowpanes. "And sometimes I wonder if that quiet is supposed to be filled with something—or someone—new."

"You mean someone special?" Suzie asked, grinning knowingly.

Nora blushed. "Maybe. I'm starting to think God and Santa are in cahoots and they've both forgotten my address."

Suzie laughed, squeezing her hand. "Don't underestimate

divine timing, my friend. Love has a funny way of showing up when you least expect it—and sometimes in the most inconvenient ways."

Nora lifted a brow. "Like, say, in a snowstorm?"

"Exactly," Suzie said, her voice laced with teasing wisdom. "Now drink your cider and stay off the roads until it lets up, okay?"

"I should probably get going." Nora smiled into her mug, letting the warmth spread through her palms. "I'll be careful," she promised. Then quietly, almost to herself, she added, "But maybe I'll keep an eye out for a little Christmas miracle, just in case."

A burst of laughter rose from the other side of the room, and for a fleeting moment, the weight in Nora's chest lifted. Maybe Suzie was right—maybe miracles happened when you least expected them. Still, as she slipped on her coat and glanced at the frosted panes in the door, she noticed the wind had picked up, shaking the wreaths and other porch decorations. She drew in a breath, squared her shoulders, and told herself everything would be fine.

Paying more attention to the weather might have been a good idea, though, Nora.

But she'd not missed a holiday open house at Sweet Hart Inn since Suzie and her husband Brad hosted it the first year they were married—and she really didn't want to miss this one.

There would be a silent auction later that evening, with the proceeds going to Miss Leinie's Place, a local family shelter. The community hosted many events to support the shelter, and Suzie's holiday open house was one of them. The shelter provided services for children and families—mostly for foster kids and those at risk, but also for anyone in need. Earlier today, Nora had dropped off a half-dozen boxes of gently used children's books for Christmas presents. She had also donated a new set of Christmas picture books for Suzie's silent auction.

Nora loved Harbor Falls and wanted nothing more than to be an integral part of the community—personally and business-wise.

She'd moved into town from the farm after graduating from college with a degree in library science and had taken over the family bookstore. She'd grown up out in the county, on the other side of Dalton Springs, and although she loved country life, found that she also liked the convenience of small-town living—especially after experiencing bigger city college life in central Ohio.

Columbus, in fact. The Ohio State University.

Which was actually an incredibly rewarding experience, and one she was glad she'd had—*Go Bucks!* But now, she was extremely happy and content living in her small-town mountain world.

It was also fun since she and Suzie are good friends now. And, because her best friend, Becca—who had also grown up, and still lived, in Harbor Falls—had finally stopped talking about moving away now that she'd married Sam Ackerman.

Of course, Harbor Falls was where Sam's brother, Nora's ex-boyfriend, Jack Ackerman, also lived. Keyword 'ex' boyfriend. The 'ex' boyfriend, who had recently married his high school sweetheart, Jasmine—an Atlanta attorney who moved back to Harbor Falls unexpectedly and now managed Miss Leinie's Place. All that happened a few months ago, not long, actually, after Jack and Nora broke up.

But she was over that now.

Mostly.

She glanced over at the happy couple and smiled. Jasmine grinned and waved back.

Nora knew they were happy. She could tell, and actually, she was thrilled for them.

It wasn't so much that she missed Jack. She missed being part of a couple. One day, perhaps she'd find her own true love. She'd even hired Suzie Hart once as a matchmaker!

But that didn't pan out, of course.

Maybe Santa would grant her wish this year. She'd been a good girl. Pretty much. She'd even prayed on it, but it seemed God hadn't thought it was time for her.

Yet.

She remained hopeful.

But not this Christmas. True love for her this Christmas would likely not happen. Especially since Christmas was simply hours away.

An hour later, Nora gripped the steering wheel of her shiny new red Camaro and leaned forward, as if pushing her face closer to the windshield would actually help her see better. The visibility was awful. In fact, worse than awful. The weatherman on the radio called it near whiteout conditions.

She had no business being out in this mess—in her shiny new red Camaro or in any vehicle. She should have headed out hours ago, quietly excusing herself and citing the weather. She *should* have called her father and told him she was on her way and would be at his home in Dalton Springs in time for Christmas Eve dinner—but she didn't.

And she should have double-checked her purse for her cell phone before leaving the inn.

Of course, she knew right where it was, sitting on Suzie Hart Matthews' side table in the living room. How could she forget it?

But she didn't do any of those things.

A host of other *should-haves* ran through her head.

Should have checked the weather.
Should have worn boots rather than heels.
Should have stayed home in Harbor Falls.

But no. She had to be the social butterfly and flit from one holiday scene to another, because that's what Nora Patterson does. Flit. Be social. Still, she should have taken precautions. Besides, her father was expecting her, and she didn't want to disappoint him. The days were lonely for him since her mother had passed earlier in the year.

"Please, God, just get me get to Dad's. I can't walk in snow in these shoes if I get stranded." Besides, her legs were freezing.

Should have worn pants.

If it hadn't been that she was having such a great time at Suzie's, she wouldn't have lost track of time. It was just that something was missing from her life of late, and being around people was comforting and rather soothing—if not just downright healing.

Especially this time of year.

The conversation with Suzie about her mom lingered on the fringes. Her first Christmas without her mom—it wouldn't be easy. She'd tried not to dwell on it. And she knew her father tried hard not to dwell on it too. But Christmas had been her mom's favorite time of the year and with a flick of her finger, she got them all involved in the decorating, the craft-making, the cookie-baking, the singing and movie-watching, and all the other holiday festivities.

Her mother loved to decorate, cook, and volunteer in the community—and often all of those things came together with a super-charged holiday bang! Giving back, she used to say. It's what we do. Why not do it with gusto?

"God, I miss her so much. I hope you can keep up with her up there!"

Her wipers made a less-than-perfect swipe across her icing

up windshield, and suddenly, Nora wished she could beam herself home with a wink and a nod.

"Just get me home to Dad, God. Santa. Someone. He needs me tonight."

And who do you need, Nora? It was like the voice came to her from out of nowhere.

She lifted her gaze into the shadowy snowy night again. Since she was talking to somewhat invisible beings, then why not just put it all out there?

"Come on, Santa, and God, and anyone else out there who is listening—" she leaned forward again and peered up into the darkening sky, "Time to work some Christmas magic. If you plan to bring me a future husband for Christmas this year, times a-wastin'. It's Christmas Eve already..."

That's who I need. A partner. A husband. Dare I wish?

She sighed. From her lips to God's ears, but she had her doubts.

"But I'd really be happy if you just got me safely to the farm."

Shaking her head, she concentrated on her driving and wished she were back at Suzie's.

As usual, her friend's home was warm and welcoming. A fire lit up the hearth in the living room. Cinnamon sticks and dried orange peel added a holiday zip to the house coffee blend, which not only smelled but tasted heavenly on this blustery day. She wished she had a cup of that yummy coffee right now—not to mention cookies. She had sampled more than her share of Suzie's Christmas confections. Plus, the Jam Cake with gooey caramel glaze was nearly sinful—the thick slice she'd devoured later in the afternoon had made her happy and cozy.

She'd just have to keep that warm memory in her head until she got to her dad's place.

Nora licked her lips just thinking about it. She'd definitely stayed too long. Suzie had even wanted her to spend the night.

Should have spent the night.

With the back of her gloved hand, she attempted to wipe away condensation building up on the inside of her windshield and wondered if her defroster wasn't working properly. Squinting, she cranked up the heat and peered out the hole. Her headlamps made two funnels of light pushing out in front of the car, with a snow-sleet mixture slanting into the beam.

A knot curled in her stomach. She had about a thirty-minute drive to her father's home—on a good day, and this wasn't a good day. Even though she didn't have to go over Falls Mountain, she had to go through the foothills and around the lake. The road was narrow and curvy in places. The evening was only going to get darker and the snow deeper. Never in her life had she seen the white stuff come down so hard and so fast. With dusk falling and the snow, the visibility was getting worse. The ruts in the road looked at least a couple of inches deep already.

Ruts. Someone had come this way before her, not very long ago. Some other fool, she guessed. Then, just as she had that thought, she saw the brake lights flash in front of her, like someone was intentionally pushing a foot on and off the brake, warning her to—

Stop?!

She slammed on her own brakes, gripped the steering wheel tighter, and braced herself.

"Not. Gonna!"

The Camaro fishtailed, and its back end slid to the right, swinging around and clipping the tail end of the vehicle in the road. She spun again and shrieked, losing all sense of direction, the car moving of its own accord. By then she had released the steering wheel and covered her face with her hands.

Sweet Jesus, take the wheel!

With a crunch of metal against something super solid, the vehicle came to an abrupt, jolting halt. Nora's body thrust to the left, and her head cracked against the driver's side window. Pain shot through her temple, and then just as quickly as it had all started, her world went black.

———

REVEREND ROCKFORD PETERS NEARLY CURSED when his old Chevy Blazer stalled on Lake Road at the foot of Falls Mountain. *Nearly cursed* being the operative words. He wasn't averse to slewing an occasional *expletive deleted* when the timing was right, and he was alone, and the situation warranted it—but he tried like heck to rein in those expletives when he could because he didn't want to let one slip in front of his parishioners. He had a reputation to uphold, after all.

He stared at the flat-lined bars on his cell phone, and his stomach sank. He knew the general vicinity of where he was, but the storm had disoriented him a little. He'd been heading back home after attending an afternoon service near Asheville to put the finishing touches on his own candlelight service at the Methodist Church in Harbor Falls, when his bald tires had skidded on the slick mush.

Should have bought new tires before winter. But he'd spent that money on Christmas gifts for the foster kids' party at Miss Leinie's place. Jasmine Walker Ackerman had been more than appreciative, and the smiles on the kids' faces had warmed his heart.

That was worth it—even though he was temporarily inconvenienced right now.

Next paycheck, new tires. He mentally put that on his to-do list. In the meantime, he would keep those warm smiles on

9

his mind as he figured out how to get through the next few hours and get home.

The cold front had raced over the mountain unexpectedly, leaving in its wake a mess of freezing rain, followed by sleet and a pelting snowstorm. And right about now, with his right tire off the edge of the road, and the back end of his vehicle sticking out cockeyed over the two-lane, he wanted to spit out the most satisfying expletive he could muster. Preferably one that started and ended with a hard consonant sound.

Lights in his rearview mirror caught his eye.

He pumped his brakes. "Dammit!"

The car behind him slid sideways, from what he gathered as he watched its headlights arc off the mountain wall. The vehicle's passenger side slammed into his rear end and pushed the Blazer further onto the shoulder. The Chevy rocked a bit, and he held his breath, not ready to ride this thing down the small slope he feared was there. He watched the lights behind him spin again and twist back the other way, heard another screeching crash, and then silence.

He sat there for a moment, unsure of his next move. The only sounds were the ice pellets hitting his windshield and an increasing creaking noise coming from somewhere underneath his vehicle.

Too quiet. What about the people in the other car? He heard nothing, and that concerned him.

Fishing a flashlight out from under his seat, he pushed open the driver's side door and stepped out into the weather. An icy blast cut into his face as he stood. He narrowed his gaze and glanced behind his truck. The other car's lights were still on; the beams aimed toward the trees to his left. The snow was coming down thick and heavy now, already building up on the roof of the red sports car. He stepped toward the vehicle and flashed his light, the beam landing on the driver's side window. His stomach clenched when he saw the smear of blood on the glass and a mass of long blond hair.

"Damn. I mean, oh good Lord. Please help her." *Maybe this is why I'm here.*

He rushed as best he could through the slush toward the woman and lifted the door latch. The door opened, and she fell like dead weight toward the ground. With a combination of what he supposed was pure adrenaline and sheer determination, he caught her up and lifted her into his arms. Her head fell back, slack. Her eyes closed. Her red lipstick-stained lips slightly parted.

Rock looked into her face, heaved in a deep breath, and shifted her body to where her face was nestled snug against his chest, and out of the driving wind. He didn't recognize the woman. She definitely was not one of his parishioners. He also knew she needed help. *His* help. And he had to see that she got it.

He straightened and stared at his surroundings. Snow. Trees. He knew the mountain and rocks were behind him, but he could barely see past the wet snow curtaining his view. Briefly, he closed his eyes. "Please, God, show me the way. Oh, and sorry about those two expletives."

He opened his eyes again. The snow slowly let up. As best he could, he played the flashlight over the scene and scanned the horizon. Trees. More trees. And there. A mailbox. Or the remnants of one, at least. The post was bent, and the box itself was on the ground, but at least it was evidence of a residence there at some point, past or present.

Right?

Beside the post, there appeared to be a break in the tree line.

A lane? A gravel drive leading somewhere?

"I'll take that," he whispered. "Thank you." As if warning him not to linger, a gust of snow blew up into his face, cold and wet, and temporarily blinding him. "I'm moving, Lord. Just let me get her safe and warm."

Carefully, he slipped the flashlight into his pocket, the beam shining up into the night. Enough to light his way. For now. He started toward the mailbox, snow slanting into his face. Once he got into the clearing and headed back through the trees, the snow dissipated somewhat, but the wind cut right through him. The woman grew heavier in his arms, but he refused to think about that, and kept putting one foot straight in front of the other.

Step after step, after step.

One leap of faith at a time.

When he thought he could go no further, when his knees were about to buckle and he could no longer feel his hands, he shuffled a few steps more and hit something solid with the toe of his boot.

He blinked and stared down through watery, stinging eyes. A porch step.

He glanced up. A cabin.

Thank You.

Chapter Two

A n old cord of wood lay in a wooden box next to the stone fireplace. With the aid of the flashlight, Rock quickly checked the damper and shone the light up into the chimney. He prayed no birds had nested there, or that there'd be any other problems with it. Who knew how long it had been since the thing had been used? He stacked a few pieces of the wood and kindling just so, and crumbled up a few pages from an old hunting magazine. He found matches, cold but dry, conveniently in a matchbox on the mantel, which was both a good sign and a godsend. Within minutes, the dry wood and paper took off, flames licked higher, and the smoke rolled up the chimney.

Good. He stared into the fire until perspiration popped from his forehead.

As the first sparks caught and the fire began to build, Rock leaned one forearm on the mantel and let his breath even out. The flickering light painted the rough walls in gold and shadow, and the crackle of wood filled the silence that had followed him for years.

He wasn't used to being with people outside of church.

For as long as he could remember, his holidays were quiet—a few hours at the church, a pot of soup simmering on the stove, an empty parsonage waiting when the candles burned low. He'd tell himself the solitude didn't bother him, that his work was enough. But for a while now, even his faith had felt stretched thin around the edges.

Maybe he'd missed something along the way. Maybe he'd poured himself so deeply into other people's lives that he'd forgotten what it meant to build his own.

That's why when he'd transferred to Harbor Falls, he'd renewed an older tradition—the Christmas Eve midnight candlelight service—the one he was likely going to be AWOL from that evening.

No matter. Perhaps he was being called in an entirely different direction.

His gaze shifted to the woman on the sofa, her pale hair spilling over the old quilt. She was a stranger, but there was something about the way she breathed—steady now, peaceful—that stirred something in him. A reminder that God's plans rarely made sense at the start.

Rock blew out a slow breath and raked a hand through his damp hair. "You've got a strange sense of humor, Lord," he murmured, glancing upward. "If this is Your idea of keeping me company on Christmas Eve, You might've just outdone Yourself."

The fire popped, sparks spiraling upward like tiny stars. He smiled faintly.

"Still... Thank You for getting her here. For getting us both here."

Then, with a quiet sigh, he turned back to the task at hand, determined to keep her safe until morning.

He drew in one more steady breath, letting the warmth of the flames chase away the last of the mountain chill—and the heaviness that had been sitting on his chest all evening. Duty called him back to the present. Whatever questions weighed on his heart could wait.

Right now, there was a woman who needed him.

NORA GROANED. HER BODY SHIFTED AND THEN rolled onto something lumpy. A dull throbbing pain radiated through her forehead and around to the back of her head. She tried to blink but found that one simple action difficult, and with each effort to flutter her eyelids open, she failed.

Cold. So cold.

She had a vague remembrance of someone. Of being held and maybe carried. Of wind, sharp and biting. Of an occasional deep voice saying things like, "I'll take care of you," and "We'll get you warm soon. Promise." Of her hands and legs shaking and then going numb.

Then nothing else until now.

She curled onto her side seeking warmth and found some by burrowing deeper into something scratchy. Didn't matter. Her face was warmer now. Her legs and hands tingled, and that made all the difference in the world. Tingling meant she was alive. Right?

Her brain fuzzy, she felt disoriented, but the warmth cloaked her inside a happy place for a moment—then she faded back into a black void.

WORRIED DIDN'T BEGIN TO DESCRIBE ROCK'S concern for the woman. As she nuzzled into the crevice made between the back and bottom cushions of the old sofa, he covered her with a quilt he found on the small bed in the corner. It wasn't the cleanest blanket he'd ever seen—although he gave it a good shake to get the dust off—but it provided warmth and comfort, and right now, that was the most important thing.

The woman barely moved during their trek through the woods other than an occasional incoherent mumble against his chest or snuggling closer to find warmth. Her eyelids had fluttered once or twice when he'd tucked the quilt around her. He needed to tend to her injuries, but first, they'd needed heat, and he saw to that quickly.

Stepping back, he surveyed his surroundings, flashing the light in his hand about the room. They had stumbled upon an old cabin—probably a hunting cabin—and one that hadn't been used for a while. He'd shouldered his way through the door and a rusty lock. Fortunately, the structure was sturdy and weatherproof, breaking the driving, icy wind. No whistling noises came through the walls either.

He'd take that blessing.

Setting the flashlight on the table, he sloughed out of his bulky overcoat. Caked snow and ice fell to the wooden plank floor. He parked the coat over a metal kitchen chair and shined the flashlight about to locate a broom, then swept the ice away toward the door to avoid puddles later. He'd keep the fire going in the fireplace, situated opposite the sofa, for as long as he possibly could. The wood stack inside was meager, at best, and while he was certain there'd be a bigger wood pile outside, he wasn't too keen on searching for it at the moment.

They'd do with what they had inside. Certainly, he could find things to burn if it came to it. The flashlight battery wouldn't last forever, he knew, and they needed both the heat and light from the fire to get through the night.

But first, the woman. Still drowsy and semi-conscious, she faced the back cushions of the old sofa. Sitting on the edge, he leaned over to study her face, playing the light over her. She seemed to breathe evenly, without effort. That was good. With a cold and trembling hand, he brushed her long, silky hair back from her face. She moaned and moved a little at his touch. Perhaps that was good too; she was somewhat aware of his being there.

He paused and waited, then smoothed her hair back more to reveal a bump and contusion on the side of her head. Blood matted her hair. He frowned and inspected the cut, deciding to leave it alone until he could find something to clean it with —if he'd be fortunate enough to find a first aid kit.

Huffing out a breath, he rose and slowly scanned the cabin. He prayed the fireplace would work properly and keep them warm throughout the night—it could be a long one, and he hoped just the one. The way the snow was coming down earlier, however, he feared they could be there for a while.

He certainly hoped they weren't snowbound for days. Of course, it was a blessing to be out of the weather—they had shelter; things could be worse. He'd think about other provisions, like first aid, and food, and water, later.

The woman moaned and twisted toward the crevice, mumbling something about Christmas. He smiled at that.

Pretty.

She was an attractive young woman. Younger than him, likely. It was a shame about the bump and bruise marring her looks—but that was temporary. Her features were pert and cute, yet she was womanly and, yes, quite pleasing to the eye.

Standing, he gazed down and then turned to his task. *Not thinking about how pretty she is. Work to do. You're the man, take care of things.*

Returning to the fire, he stoked it with a rusty poker leaning against the stone, and added a few more pieces of kindling.

With the task done, he turned again toward the young woman. He wished he knew who she was, but her face wasn't familiar. He knew most everyone around Harbor Falls, so that was surprising. Perhaps she was just passing through. But why she'd be out on that narrow and winding road during a snowstorm, though, he couldn't fathom—unless she was heading someplace specific. To someone or somewhere along that route.

"Probably the same reason you were," he chided, talking to himself. Like him, she may have been oblivious to the weather or had lingered too long somewhere, thinking the storm would blow over or skirt the other side of the mountain as it often does.

No such luck.

"It's Christmas Eve. Where were you heading? And who is missing you right now?"

For a moment, he wondered exactly when he would be missed and frowned that there was no one home to miss him. He'd been alone for years, his parents gone, and him an only child. At thirty-five, men his age were usually married with children. He'd not yet found the woman to fit into his life—as a wife to him, or mother to his future children—although he had spent a lot of time lately wondering if he ever would.

When would someone discover that he was missing?

Who would come looking for him?

And when?

Maybe once the parishioners had gathered for the midnight service? Or sooner?

He didn't know, and at any rate, he was giving in because he would not be getting home tonight to deliver the midnight service. Maybe then, someone would come looking.

He sat on the edge of the sofa and dragged the woman into a sitting position, tugging at her now wet coat to remove it, and then tossing it aside. He frowned, realizing that a bit of the caked-on snow had melted into the cushions and quilt—which were also now wet. She moaned and turned toward him

—blinked and shivered—then gave him a brief, blank stare. Just as quickly, her head fell slack again, onto his chest.

Rock lifted her away from the wet sofa and carried her closer to the fireplace, which warmed the room nicely. Now that her coat was off, he positioned her on the floor and did a quick assessment of her injuries—he'd once worked as a chaplain in a hospital and had witnessed emergency room triage on more than one occasion. Not that he was a doctor or anything, but he felt certain he could assess broken bones—and to his knowledge, she had none of those. No other cuts or bruising either, he found out. Just the bump on the head.

He glanced at her feet. One small foot was missing a red high-heeled shoe, and he did not know when that had happened. It could have gotten lost at any point along the way, although the scrap of leather wouldn't have provided her much protection in this weather anyway.

He smiled—women—and tried not to look at her delicate ankles.

She coughed, and then her entire body shook. Rock raced back and grabbed a few more of the covers from the bed and returned to her. He dragged an overstuffed chair closer to the fire, then pulled the woman onto his lap and wrapped them both in the covers like an overstuffed burrito. With her head nestled in the crook between his neck and chin, he tucked the blankets tightly around her feet and legs and wrapped his arms around her. He held her close, then leaned back against the chair and closed his eyes.

His last thought before contemplating sleep was that body heat was a wonderful thing.

Chapter Three

N ora blinked and sucked in a breath, inhaling a spicy scent. Umm, nice.

Aftershave. *What?*

Her eyes shot fully open, and she scrambled backwards, pushing off a man's firm chest and getting tangled in something confining, and then finally breaking free and landing firmly on her bottom on the floor. In two seconds flat, she realized she had no earthly idea where she was, or who the man was sitting two feet away, staring and reaching for her.

Also, she was hot. Sweaty.

Oh, my God. What have I been doing?

Pain shot across her forehead, and she winced. A hand went to her temple.

"Who are you? Where am I?" Her chest heaved, sucking in and blowing out breaths. She stared at the dark-haired man gawking back. His face held a startled look, as if he'd just been awakened from sleep. Her gaze scanned the room behind him, and her fuzzy brain suddenly became a little sharper.

"Where are we?" she repeated. "Why am I here? What am I *doing*?" She glanced down. "And where are my shoes?"

The man ran his hands over his face and peered back. Finally, he spoke. "That's a lot of questions. Which one do you want me to answer first?"

"All of them."

He cleared his throat and sat up straighter. "All right then. Let's see if I can get this right. I'm Reverend Rock Peters. We're in a hunting cabin because our cars crashed in the snow —that's two answers there. And you've been sleeping. I have no clue where your shoe is. Sorry."

Snow. Car. Her brain spun with remembrance. Oh my, yes. Leaving Suzie's. The car sliding, and... Then nothing. "Sleeping?"

"Yes."

"And trying to get warm, actually."

She looked down at herself. Her white blouse was damp and sticking to her chest. Damn, but if her white lacy bra wasn't showing through, like she was a contestant in a wet T-shirt contest. "But I'm all sweaty." She looked at his chest. "And so are you."

"And you are implying?"

What? What am I implying? Her brain was a little scrambled. She tilted her chin up and rubbed her forehead. "Sorry, I'm a little confused. Not implying anything, just making sure that there has been no hanky-panky going on here, because buster, if there has...."

He chuckled. "The fireplace really heated things up in this small cabin. I assure you, all we've been doing is sleeping. I'm an honorable man. You're safe with me. There has been no hanky-panky."

Nora exhaled. She glanced at the pool of blankets on the floor between them. "Then why... Why were we wrapped up in those blankets together if it's so damned hot in here?"

Wait. The man—what did he say his name was? Reverend? She really shouldn't be cursing.

Oh shit. *Shoot!*

The Reverend stood. "I wasn't doing anything. You weren't doing anything. We were trying to get warm. That's it. I assure you, Miss—I'm sorry, but I don't know your name—"

"Nora. Nora Patterson." She put out her hand, feeling awkward. This wasn't a business meeting after all. It was... Hell, *heck*, what was it?

He shook it. His hand was warm and smooth. "Miss Nora —it is Miss, isn't it?"

Nora nodded. Slowly. Oh, hells bells. Is he coming on to her?

"Yes..." She drew the word out slowly, wondering whether she should even have uttered it at all.

What was she thinking? Of course, he was not coming on to her. He was a man of the cloth. Just being kind. Definitely not making a pass. He hadn't even indicated that he found her attractive.

Why would she even think of that?

In any other situation, she might find him attractive, though. Not that she didn't find him attractive now—dark hair, chiseled features, obviously fit and took care of himself. Handsome.

Okay, so I find him attractive. Even though I am not sure what is going on here.

He nodded back. "All right then, Miss Nora. I assure you I have been a perfect gentleman, and you have been a lady." He paced a little, right, then left. "When we arrived here, we were nearly frozen and snow-covered, and you were unconscious. I knew I had to get both of us warm, or we might not survive the night. That fireplace puts out quite a bit of heat, which actually, I am quite thankful for, seeing that we're caught in a snowstorm and who knows when we'll get out of here."

Nora blinked again. "We're stranded?" Not only was she in a strange place, with a strange man, but she couldn't leave?

"Appears that may be the case. I'd say we'll know more come morning and daylight. By the way, how does your head feel?"

Nora's hand went to her forehead again. "Hurts like hell. *Heck.*"

The Reverend smiled and nodded. "Seems it hasn't affected your speech."

Nora didn't hesitate. "I talk a lot, especially when I am nervous. Sorry, Mr., er, Reverend, er, I didn't catch your first name."

"Rock."

"Rock?"

"Yes."

"Oh."

He smiled then and sat in the chair. "My mother loved Rock Hudson. Actually, my given name is Rockford, but Reverend Rockford Peters is a mouthful. You can call me Rock or Reverend Peters. Whichever you prefer."

Nora felt her eyes widen. Whatever I prefer? She stood and faced the fire, putting a little distance between them. Calling him Rock seemed way too intimate. She stared into the flames. "Reverend Peters is probably a good place to start."

She heard him rise and take a few steps behind her. "That's absolutely fine, Miss Patterson."

Nora turned and watched him head out the cabin door. The wind and a blast of snow shot inside the small room as he stepped out onto the porch, bending to get something. Behind her, the fireplace flared, warming her backside. She edged away from the hearth.

Panic raced from her gut to her throat. *OMG. What is he doing?*

She pushed to her feet and started for the door. "Where are you going? Stop! Please don't leave me here alone!"

ROCK TURNED AS HE HEARD NORA'S SHOUT. He looked back through the door in time to see her toes catch on the edge of the rug, and her entire body lurch forward. He watched as if in slow motion, as she dove forward and took a header off the arm of the couch, and then rolled to the floor and moaned.

He dropped the bowl of snow he had just scooped up and raced back into the room, slamming the door shut behind him.

"Nora!"

She rolled onto her side, pushing herself into a sitting position. "I'm usually not this clumsy," she muttered.

He helped her up by cradling her elbows in his hands. "Are you okay?"

She stared at him and blinked. "I'm a klutz."

"No, you're still a bit disoriented."

"Yes. My head is fizzy. Uh, fuzzy."

"Were you dizzy?"

"Yes. I meant dizzy." Grimacing, she glanced off. "I think I was dizzy before I tripped. Or maybe it was just a plain stupid air trip."

Rock grinned. He couldn't help himself. "Well, here is the thing. You've had a nice whack on your head, and you need to stay put unless I'm helping you get somewhere. Let's get you over to that chair."

She frowned and then fixed her gaze on his face. "Actually, I think I want to sit right here. What were you doing? Leaving me?" She paused, her eyes searching. "Please don't leave me. I don't know how to keep the fire going, and I don't feel well, and...."

Rock silenced her with a forefinger to her lips. He hadn't intended to do that, but it was the only way he figured he could stop her from talking. The second he touched her soft lips with the pad of his finger though, he regretted it. A spark traveled from the tip to his heart. And the dewy look in her eyes staring back hooked him in to seal the deal.

He couldn't deny any longer the attraction he felt toward her. Which was utterly stupid, of course. They'd just met, and this wasn't real life, and she was barely even coherent. But he had watched her for what seemed like hours when she was out. He'd been worried about her with every whimper that stirred her plump lips. He'd watched her with concern and empathy and had prayed he'd done the right thing by bringing her here. And then while holding her in his arms as they slept, he'd felt a strange sort of rightness—a warmth in his heart, which he was sure he'd never felt before.

Through all of that, yes, he'd started feeling some sort of pull toward her.

Nonsense, his brain lectured. It's the situation. Don't confuse things.

He drew back and put his hand in his lap. He wished his brain wasn't so practical sometimes. Still, he stared into her eyes. "Nora, I wasn't leaving you. I wouldn't. I was going out to get some snow to melt to clean the blood off your forehead. I'm sorry. I should have said that, but I didn't want to alarm you about the blood." Her gaze continued to penetrate, and he knew he had to make a choice—drown in those enormous eyes of hers, or back away.

She touched her temple again. "Oh," she whispered. "I didn't realize. It's just confusing."

He didn't budge. The softness of her small voice kept him glued to the floor beside her. "I understand."

"I'm so stupid," she said.

"No, you're not. I should have told you what I was doing."

"Is there a lot of blood?"

He brushed back a few wayward tendrils and re-inspected

the wound. "It's dried and clotting, but yeah, there is a fair amount of blood. Want me to take care of it?"

She nodded, catching his stare. "Please?"

He smiled again and watched her lips curl up slightly. "Don't move. I'll be right back."

Rock begrudgingly pulled away and headed for the door. He wrestled with it against the wind, then glanced back and realized her gaze was on him. Suddenly, he felt a million miles away from her, and he did not like that feeling. Quickly, he located the bowl, scooped up some snow, and headed back inside toward the fire.

He set the metal bowl on the hearth and waited for the snow to melt while he went off in search of a cloth. All the while, without even looking, he knew Nora's eyes were following him every step of the way.

Chapter Four

Becca North Ackerman stared out the window the farmhouse she lived in with her husband, Sam, and listened to the empty, endless ringtone in her ear that came from Nora's phone. The snow was piling up outside, and her best friend was not answering her cell. Neither scenario boded well, nor did the sinking feeling in the pit of her gut. The worry was almost more than she could stand.

"Did she answer?"

Becca clicked off the phone, turned to her husband, and shook her head. "Something's wrong. I can feel it." Her phone rang, and she glanced down and added, "Crap. It's Nora's dad again. He's frantic, and I don't know what to say to him." She let the phone ring, and it stopped after five rings.

Sam stepped closer and touched her arm. "Call him back and see if you can calm him down. We're going to have to go looking, you know."

Breathing deeply and then exhaling, Becca met his gaze and smiled. This man of hers—he was a good man. How did she get so lucky? "I know. Are you sure you don't mind? It's a terrible night out there."

"All the more reason to get started." Wrapping his arms around her, he tugged her tight and smiled. "Nora is a pain in the ass sometimes, but you know I'd do anything for her—and you. Besides, the storm is not due to let up within the next few hours, and we need to find her sooner rather than later."

Becca hated to admit how worried she was. With a half-smile, she gave her husband a peck on the cheek and pulled back. "I'll call Mr. Patterson back now."

"I'll rally the troops," Sam said.

Turning away, Becca took a deep breath. Before punching the screen to dial Nora's father, she glanced at the clock over the fireplace mantel. It was after nine o'clock, the snow was coming down hard, and the night was pitch black. Nora hadn't been heard from since she left Suzie's, and Becca had a feeling deep in the pit of her stomach that was unsettling.

She had no clue what she was going to say to Mr. Patterson.

She dialed anyway.

"Hello!" His voice was urgent, unsteady.

"Mr. Patterson. It's Becca. I'm sorry I missed your call."

"That's okay. Any news?"

Becca frowned to herself, hating to disappoint him. "I'm afraid not, but Sam is getting ready to go look for her. He'll probably take Jack with him and others."

"I'll meet you wherever you want."

The last thing Becca wanted was Nora's father out in this storm, too. "Oh no, Mr. Patterson. Stay there in case she makes it home to you. Okay? You stay put. That way, I'll also know how and where to reach you. You just have a landline, right?"

"Yes, that's right."

"I'm staying here. I'll be your contact, okay? And I'll keep you informed every step of the way. Sam and I have cell phones and two-way radios, so we'll keep in constant contact."

The response from the other end of the phone was a long and worried sigh. She knew it had been a rough year for him, and for Nora, with her mother passing so suddenly several months ago.

After a moment, Becca added, "Sam will find her, Mr. Patterson. I promise. There is only one route between Sweet Hart Inn and your farm, so they know where to look."

"That damn foothills road worries me."

Becca had had the same thought. "Perhaps she stopped somewhere safe and her phone battery died. We will figure it out. I promise!"

He didn't immediately respond, then finally said, "I hope so. I just hope it's not too late."

Becca didn't like to view the glass half-empty, but she hoped for the same thing. "Sam and Jack will find her soon. I'm sure of it."

SUZIE PUSHED THROUGH HER BACK DOOR WHILE carrying her son, Petey. She paused for a moment just inside, hearing something. There. A phone ringing? "What in the world?" She glanced at Brad, who was shutting the kitchen door behind them against the wind and driving snow. "That's not our landline," she said.

Brad's eyebrows knit. "A cell phone ringing?"

"Sounds like it. I wonder whose though?"

"Here, give me Petey," Brad said. "I'll take him upstairs and get him into bed. You go see what that's all about."

The ringing stopped.

Handing over their child, Suzie smiled. "Dad wore his little butt out."

Brad laughed. "Yeah, he told me he was going to make sure

Petey fell asleep quickly tonight so we could get all the last-minute gifts wrapped and assembled."

Suzie didn't want to think about that just yet but was glad that at least they were going to have more time. With the storm, they had foregone the Christmas Eve midnight service at the church and stayed inside instead. That's why they went to get Petey, who had stayed the day with her parents, as their last guest left for the evening.

The cell phone rang again.

"Someone left their phone behind," Suzie said.

"More than likely."

She jogged off toward the front of the house and scanned the living room. The ring was coming from the area of the sofa, but she didn't immediately see it. Moving closer, she noticed it tucked between a cushion and the side arm. "There you are." She fished it out of the sofa, looked at the illuminated face, and frowned at who was calling. "Becca?"

She pushed the button. "Hello?"

"Oh, thank God. Nora?"

"No, this is Suzie. Becca, is that you?"

"Yes! Where is Nora?"

"She's not here, Becca, but she must have left her phone behind. What's going on?"

Suzie heard a tremendous sigh come through from the opposite end. "Nora is missing, Suzie. And I guess this explains why she wasn't answering her phone. She must have left it at your house."

"Missing?"

"She didn't show up at her dad's. She should have been there hours ago."

Suzie turned and watched Brad descend the stairwell to her right. "What can we do?" Brad must have sensed something because his face suddenly looked worried. He approached her and touched her elbow. Suzie put Becca on speakerphone.

"Sam and Jack are getting ready to head out. Nora is probably somewhere between here and her father's house, but she has to travel Lake Road to get there, and then around the mountain, of course. Can they meet at your place to group up and form a strategy?"

"Absolutely," Brad interrupted. "I'll go with them."

"Might be good if there were two trucks," Becca offered.

Brad reached into his pocket. "I'll call Matt. I'll also find out if there is any information from the local police department, road conditions and such, and make sure they know Nora is missing."

"Great," Becca said. "Sam will be there in twenty minutes, hopefully. It may take a bit to get down off the mountain."

Suzie bristled. "Tell him just to be careful!"

"We'll talk soon. You stay put so we can be command central. Okay?"

"You got it." She hit the button to end the call. "Oh my, Brad. We have to find her. Nora is not equipped to take on a snowstorm! I feel so bad. I should not have let her leave, but she insisted!"

"I know. What's done is done. Can't worry about that now." He leaned in to kiss her nose. "We will find her. I'm going to go warm up the truck and de-ice."

"Be careful, Brad."

"I will."

"I love you."

He kissed her again. "I love you too, baby."

About fifteen minutes later, Suzie watched from her living room window as Jack and Sam's sturdy landscaping truck made its way to the end of her driveway. Her brother-in-law, Matt Branson, a Harbor Falls police officer, had arrived a few minutes earlier in his four-wheel-drive pickup. He and Brad sat in the truck at the edge of the road waiting. Suzie knew Matt would have his police radio with him to keep in touch with the local police departments. Hopefully, by now there were others out looking too.

Her cell phone jiggled in her hand, and she glanced down to see a text from Brad.

Heading out. Decided to stay together rather than split up.

Good idea, Suzie typed. *Please be careful.*

Brad added. *Will do. Matt says Dalton Springs P.D. is heading this way on Lake Road from the opposite direction.*

"Good." Suzie let out a sigh. *Be safe.*

Always.

At that moment, she said a brief prayer for Nora and everyone else out on the road that Christmas Eve evening.

A HANDFUL OF CHURCH MEMBERS STOOD OUTSIDE the First Methodist Church of Harbor Falls, looking at the church façade, partially illuminated by streetlights. The stained-glass windows were not backlit with light. The front doors were locked.

The parishioners standing on the doorsteps chattered about the dilemma, seemingly all talking at once.

"The church is dark."

"Extremely unusual."

"Anyone call Reverend Peters?"

"Should we go on in and wait? I need to get the programs out."

"Who has the key?"

"I'm glad there is a break in the snow right now, but I don't think anyone will be coming. Do you? Should we cancel?"

"Reverend Peters has to do that."

"But where is he?"

"I should get the organ warmed up."

"I have the candles. It's nearly ten o'clock. He's usually here by now."

"Call him!"

"I did! He didn't answer."

"How long ago?"

"Oh, about twenty minutes."

"People will arrive soon."

"He's not answering. Again. Anyone try the parsonage?"

"It's dark too. Noticed that when I drove by."

"Probably in bed like the rest of us should be."

"Did he cancel? The storm is supposed to get worse, you know. I hear Nora Patterson is missing over near the mountain."

"Missing? Oh, my...."

"The weather is worse over there, according to my cousin."

"Wait. My phone is ringing."

"I just got a text message."

"Me too."

"Oh, the church hotline has been activated. The deacons are canceling the service?"

"I have a bad feeling. The deacons?"

"I'm sure it's because of the storm."

"But where is the Reverend?"

"Good question!"

"Wait. Another text from Deacon Roy."

Pause. Then a collective gasp.

"Reverend Peters is missing too?"

Chapter Five

Nora watched as Reverend Peters—Rock—hustled about in preparation to tend to her wounds. She wasn't certain if her dizziness was from the bump—or the flutter in her heart—but there was something about Reverend Rock Peters that made her all warm and tingly inside.

She shook off that thought and glanced toward the fire. It was the blow to the head. Had to be. No way could a perfect stranger make her all atwitter inside. Especially in the region of her heart.

The storm outside had quieted to a whisper, snow brushing against the old windowpanes like soft fingertips. Inside, the cabin glowed with firelight—orange and gold and alive. The air smelled of pine smoke and melted snow, and the low hiss of the flames filled the pauses between their words.

Rock shifted another log into place. "There," he said, sitting back on his heels. "That should last us for a while."

Nora tucked her legs beneath her on the sofa and hugged the quilt tighter around her shoulders. "I never realized how loud quiet can be," she murmured.

He looked over, one brow raised. "Loud?"

She nodded. "It's like... when everything stops, the quiet starts echoing all the things you try not to think about."

Rock smiled faintly. "That's more profound than most of my Sunday sermons."

Nora laughed softly, embarrassed. "Sorry. Guess I'm feeling philosophical. Storms do that."

"They do," he agreed. His voice dropped lower, thoughtful. "They stop us long enough to hear ourselves."

She studied him, intrigued by the way the light caught his eyes—warm brown with flecks of gold that mirrored the fire. "You've probably had a lot of quiet nights like this."

He hesitated, then nodded. "More than I'd like to admit. Sometimes I wonder if God made me a minister because He knew I needed people more than most—and this was His way of making sure I'd never be alone, even when I am."

Her chest tightened. "That's sad, Reverend."

"Maybe," he said with a small smile. "Or maybe it's grace in disguise."

She looked away, blinking hard. "I lost my mom this year. When I visit Dad, the house feels so empty now, even with the radio on and the lights twinkling. Tonight was supposed to be cheerful, but—" Her voice hitched, and she covered it with a nervous laugh. "I guess I didn't plan on colliding with a minister."

Rock chuckled softly. "Most people don't."

The sound of his laugh curled around her like comfort. For the first time all evening, the ache in her heart eased a little. Maybe it was the firelight, or the way his voice warmed the room, or the sudden certainty that they had found each other that night—for reasons neither could yet name.

The fire shifted with a soft sigh, and the moment folded in on itself—quiet again, comfortable. Nora wasn't sure whether the warmth in her chest came from the flames or from the man sitting across from her, his gaze steady and kind. For the first time in a long while, she didn't feel quite so alone. She drew in a slow breath, gathering her thoughts, reminding herself of who she was and what she'd promised her heart after the break-up with Jack.

While men were frequently attracted to her, it took her a while to get to know and be comfortable around men. Any man. Especially new-to-her men. And she didn't throw herself at men either. Well, not usually. Becca would likely disagree. In fact, when Nora had hired Suzie—who was also a matchmaker besides being a chef and the owner of Sweet Hart Inn—to find her a date, Nora had handled it all wrong. In all her nervousness, she'd come on way too strong, and it had backfired. Big time.

So wrong, in fact, that her date, Sam Ackerman, had gone after Becca, instead.

But that turned out great for Becca, right? She and Sam were very happy together, and she was happy for them. Her relationship with Sam's brother, Jack, however, hadn't fared so well.

Just not meant to be.

She had done her fair share of boyfriend chasing over the years, though. It was just that... Well, after Jack, she had laid low for a while, keeping to herself.

Nora sighed. Would there ever be a time when she would find someone perfect for her?

"I think I'm ready. Are you?"

Nora blinked out of her trance and looked up. Rock stood before her, his eyes twinkling, and his lips smiling. "Ready?"

For love? For you?

Stop it, Nora!

"Ready? I, uh... For?" She saw the puzzled look on his face. "I'm sorry. My head is still fizzy and I am talking in-coherently." Or thinking illogically.

He crouched in front of her and stared into her eyes. "Nora, that's understandable. Your eyes look a little dilated, and you might have suffered a slight concussion. Don't be concerned if your words don't come out right."

What about my thoughts? Can I trust them? She nodded. "Okay."

He grinned back. "So, let me see if I can clean that cut up a bit. Hmm?"

She agreed with a nod. "Yes. Of course."

Rock held the connection between them for a moment and then settled down on the floor beside her. He dipped a cloth into the water with one hand, and with the other, pushed back her hair. With careful, gentle motions, he swabbed at her forehead and scalp.

"Let me know if I put too much pressure on this," he said, his voice soft and low.

Nora closed her eyes. "It's fine. Thank you."

"Not a problem, Nora."

She kept her eyes closed, absorbing the feel of his fingertips gently swiping. The hand holding her hair back threaded through her tresses and cupped her head, holding her steady. He dabbed the area softly, slowly.

She let him do whatever he felt he needed to do.

"It's not a deep cut," he said. "Just surface, busting up the skin a bit on your scalp. There is some bruising, and you have a small knot. At least it is puffing outward and not inward. I've heard that's important, although I'm not exactly sure why. Head injuries always bleed a lot, too, making the cut look worse than it really is."

Nora exhaled. "Oh good. I guess I'll live then." She eased out a slight grin.

Rock chuckled. "Yes, I think you'll make it to another sunrise."

Sunrise meant Christmas morning here in this cabin. With

him. She was going to miss Christmas at home. So would he.

"My dad is probably worried sick."

Rock pulled back, and Nora opened her eyes. He searched her face and said, "He's waiting for you? Tell me more. Are you comfortable telling me a little about yourself, Nora? After all, it looks like we are going to be stuck here together for a while."

That panicked her a little. Not the being with him part, because she felt safe with him—but the fact that they were stranded. People didn't know where they were, the unpredictability of the storm—it was all a little unsettling. "Do you think we'll be here a long time?"

He placed a hand over hers. "I didn't mean to alarm you. I'm sorry. I think the answer to that is that we just don't know, Nora. I wish I had a better response."

He was as nervous about this as she was, she realized then.

Shrugging, she wet her suddenly dry lips. "I know. I'm still trying to sort this all out in my head. I'm sorry if I seem a little panicked and scattered."

"You seem none of the kind. This isn't an everyday situation, so even if you feel that way, it's normal!"

He grinned then, and Nora felt a little more relieved. "Thank you."

"For what?"

"For helping me to feel calm. And safe. For taking care of me."

His smile deepened, and for a moment, he studied her face.

Am I holding my breath?

"I'm pretty sure you can take care of yourself, Nora, but I'll take that and run with it. If you feel safe and secure, then I've done my job. And that makes me happy."

Nora grinned back and sighed. "I think you are a very good man, Reverend Rock."

At that, Rock Peters blushed a little.

Nora decided then to switch the subject back to safer ground. "About my father. I was on my way to have Christmas Eve dinner with him."

"He lives out this way?"

She nodded. "He lives in the house I grew up in, on a small farm outside of Dalton Springs. My mom passed earlier this year, so it's a sad time. Dad wanted to have Christmas Eve dinner together. I'm sure he's worried. And lonely. And...worried."

Rock rinsed the rag and continued gently swiping at her scalp. "Holidays without loved ones can be difficult. Depression can set in this time of year for many of us."

"I think Dad is depressed. He and Mom were so much in love."

"Long marriage?"

"Yes, and a happy one. Over forty years. I can only hope to have the same one day."

Rock dropped his hands and studied her. "I understand. I'm sure he's worried about you."

"Probably. I'm their only child, and they had me later in life. Truth is, I'm worried about him."

"Do you think he'll come looking?"

"He might. And he's not in great health, so that's another concern besides this crazy weather." She glanced off toward the fire. Then abruptly, she blurted out, "What about you? Who is waiting for you to come home?"

He paused, and Nora turned back to look at him.

"No one," he said after a moment. "I live alone."

The conversation dropped from there, and Nora felt like that was probably best. Tugging the quilt up around her chest, she closed her eyes. "I'm suddenly tired. I think I'll try to get some rest.

Rock Peters grinned warmly, even though his expression looked sad. "I think that's a wonderful idea, Nora."

Nora opened her eyes to find him studying her. "Okay, good. Well then. Thank you for taking care of the...well, the blood. I'm sure it was icky and unpleasant, and you really didn't have to do that. Suddenly, I'm not feeling so dizzy anymore, but I have a bit of a headache and am sleepy. I wonder... Should I sleep? You don't think I have a concussion. Do you?"

"Well, I'm not sure...."

"Of course, we were sleeping earlier, and I seem to be okay."

"Yes, but—"

She glanced about. *Why am I talking about sleeping?* Not a safe turn of subject. She remembered being crowded up against him under the blankets. Hot and sweaty. His aftershave teasing her awake. Would she ever get that scent out of her nose?

Sleep finally claimed her in fits and starts.

When she woke again, the world had changed.

THE STORM CALMED SOMETIME AFTER MIDNIGHT. Now, only the occasional sigh of wind pressed against the cabin walls. The fire had burned down to a low orange glow, throwing shadows that swayed like candlelight across the log walls.

Rock knew he'd have to stoke the fire again soon, and probably add another log, but Nora was sleeping so soundly, he didn't want to do anything to wake her. Rest is what she needed, and if he was honest with himself, he could use a little quiet time to contemplate a few things.

Namely, his aloneness.

He glanced her way. Of course, he wasn't alone tonight, and that was a blessing. Had she not come down that long stretch of road when she had, he could be weathering this storm on his own. And he would have, of course, but frankly, he was tired of weathering storms alone.

What would it be like to have a long partnership, a marriage like Nora's parents', to weather life's storms together? Lately, he'd nearly convinced himself that a partner to share his life with was not in the cards for him.

Not in God's plan for him.

But tonight? Now?

He looked again at the sofa and the sleeping Nora. She moaned softly and twisted under the quilt, facing him now. Gradually, her eyes blinked awake, and he sat quietly and simply watched her sleep-softened expression become aware of her surroundings.

"You're awake," he said after a moment. "I thought I'd lost you to sleep for good."

"Hard to sleep with all that racket," she teased faintly, gesturing toward the fire. "It sounds like the woods are talking."

"It does that up here in the mountains. All the old trees like to have the last word."

Nora smiled, easing upright as he handed her a chipped mug. "Is this coffee?"

"Something like it," he said. "Instant miracle in a tin. Might even qualify as holy water tonight."

She took a sip and nearly laughed. "If this is holy, I'll stick to Suzie's cinnamon blend."

Rock grinned and sat opposite her on the floor, his back against the sofa. "You know, I think I've heard half this town talk about Suzie's coffee. I should've stopped in before now."

"I'll tell her you said so. She'll probably name a blend after you."

He laughed. "Now there's a goal!"

Nora giggled along with him, and he realized he liked her bubbly giggle, very much. In fact, he'd love to hear more of it.

They sat quietly for a while, trading small smiles and listening to the storm fade. Then Nora said, almost shyly, "Speaking of goals... You know, I was thinking earlier. I own the bookstore in town, and if I ever get things just right, I want to host a community reading night. A space where people can belong, especially the ones who don't feel like they do."

He studied her face. "That sounds like ministry to me."

"Books are their own kind of gospel."

"Amen to that."

She hesitated, then asked, "What about you?"

"Me?"

"Do you have a goal?"

He thought for a moment. *Do I?* Of course he had goals, but as he sped through the filing cabinet in his brain, all he could come up with were church-related goals.

Obviously, you need to work on your personal life, Rock.

"Well?"

He studied her. "I want to continue to serve the Lord in whatever capacity he has for me to do so, Nora."

Her smile broadened. "I like that." She looked into the fire for a moment. "We're going to miss Christmas in the morning, aren't we?" She rotated back to look at him.

He wasn't in the least worried about that, because he knew he would spend Christmas morning with her—and that suited him just fine. "I think Christmas happens wherever you are, and with whomever you are with."

Their gazes caught and held again. Nora was certain she could feel his warmth.

"Do you have a favorite Christmas memory, Reverend?" she asked.

He stared into the fire. "A few years ago, I volunteered at a foster home in Asheville. We did a nativity play, but the little boy playing Joseph was so nervous he forgot his line. When I whispered it to him, he asked me if God could still find him in a storm."

Nora's throat tightened. "What did you tell him?"

Rock's voice softened. "That God does His best work in storms."

Silence settled again, comfortable this time. The fire crackled, and a few flakes of snow whispered against the window.

NORA LEFT THE SOFA, DRAGGING THE QUILT WITH her, and drifted closer to the stone fireplace. She sat cross-legged on the floor, staring into the flames that blurred as her eyes misted. "That boy sounds braver than I've felt in a while," she whispered. "I keep telling myself to have faith, but mine looks more like hope wearing borrowed shoes."

Rock smiled at that. "Hope's just faith in motion, Nora. Different shoes, same journey."

She turned her gaze toward him, blinking away a tear. "Then maybe I'm learning to walk again."

He nodded slowly. "We all are. I've spent years preaching about grace, but sometimes I think God keeps reminding me it's not a onetime gift. We get it over and over—if we're willing to take it."

Their eyes met across the firelight, an unspoken understanding passing between them. Two people who'd lost things they weren't sure they'd ever find again—both still believing, in their own ways, that redemption was possible.

The fire cracked sharply, sending a spray of sparks up the chimney. Nora startled and laughed softly, the sound easing the heaviness that had settled between them.

"I guess even the fire agrees," she said, leaning forward to nudge a log with the poker. "Keep the faith burning, right?"

Rock chuckled. "Or maybe it's reminding us not to let things burn out."

The flames flared higher, lighting up their faces in warm gold. For a few breaths, they simply sat there, listening to the wind sigh against the eaves and the rhythm of each other's quiet breathing.

Nora inhaled deeply—the air was a mix of wood smoke, coffee, and the faint scent of his aftershave that somehow hadn't faded. It all felt too intimate, too safe, and yet she didn't want to step away from it.

She rose to add another log to the fire, but when she bent to place it on the hearth, the room tilted slightly. The edges of her vision dimmed.

Rock was on his feet in an instant. "Easy there."

"I'm fine," she said with a weak laugh, steadying herself against the arm of the chair. "Guess I'm still finding my balance—in more ways than one." Maybe she'd found her footing after all.

He caught her by the elbows before she could protest, his hands firm but gentle. "That's all right, Nora. Second chances take practice."

For a long, quiet moment, neither moved. His hands stayed where they were; hers rested lightly against his wrists. She could feel his pulse under her fingertips—strong, steady, grounding her. The room seemed to hold its breath.

Finally, she drew in a slow, trembling one of her own. "Thank you," she whispered.

Rock's thumb brushed, almost by accident, over her wrist before he stepped back. "Get some rest, Nora."

She smiled faintly and returned to the sofa, tucking herself beneath the quilt once more. Outside, the snow began again— soft, steady, like a prayer answered in white, a promise of morning on its way.

Chapter Six

"I don't know about you," Mary Lou Rhodes said, turning toward the crowd gathering on the church steps, "but the weather is only going to get worse, the night darker, and all of us colder as we continue to stand here and debate this dilemma. We need to do something."

Gracie Hart Price bit her lip and looked straight at Mary Lou. "You are exactly right. We can stand here jabbering, or we can put a posse together and go out looking for those two."

"A posse? Do they even do that anymore?"

"You know what I mean, Lucki." Gracie shivered against the wind and tossed Lucki Stevenson a quick glance. "We have to help. It's what both would do. Right? You know that as well as any of us, seeing as how your marriage proposal from Dr. Sam Kirk was orchestrated by the entire town last summer."

"And by Sam, too, of course! We *are* a town that sticks together." Lucki nodded and then clamped a hand over her mouth. "Goodness. Do you think Nora and Rock are together?"

"Well, wouldn't that be romantic?" Sydney Hart elbowed

her way into the crowd, brushing snow off her shoulders. "Goodness, it's a mess out here. So glad the wind has died down some."

"Romantic?" Lucki echoed.

Sydney looked at the small throng of women. "Sure. I mean, in a snowbound romance novel kind of way, of course."

"Romantic? Hells bells!" Gracie glared at her cousin. "I know romantic—it's my business—and this isn't it. This is not good, Sydney."

Sydney crossed her arms. "Well sorry! I was just thinking that perhaps..."

Mary Lou interjected, "Look. I got it. We've all said that we wished Reverend Peters would find a wife. He's such a great guy. Does he even know Nora? She doesn't go to our church."

"But he reads a lot, so maybe he met her at the bookstore."

"Sure. The Reverend knows a lot of people in town. It's possible."

"Wouldn't it be kind of neat if they got together on this snowy and mysterious Christmas Eve?"

"Mysterious?"

"Well, sort of."

"Oh, I don't know, Mary Lou."

Gracie heaved a sigh. "Who knows and who cares? We are not getting anywhere standing about jabbering about things that don't matter right now. Let's marry the poor man off later. Right now, we need to focus. Get them both home safe and sound. You all sound like a bunch of pick-a-little, talk-a-littles."

The crowd of women stared back at her.

"What in the world are you talking about, Gracie? Pick-a-little-whats?"

Mary Lou rolled her eyes. "*Music Man*," she said. "You know, the town's gossiping women?"

"Well, I'll be...."

"Never saw that movie."

"What?"

"Let's just figure out how to find those two!"

"I wonder if anyone has contacted the police department."

"I'll check."

"Goodness y'all." Gracie motioned toward the church. "Let's stop the pick-a-littling and get inside, get warm, and make a plan."

"Excellent idea." Geraldine Weissmuller pulled a gigantic door key from her purse and reached for the door pull on the big wooden church door. She turned back before she unlocked. "Does anyone know the last time either of them were seen?"

Lucki snapped her fingers. "Good thinking, Geraldine. We need to track down their activities for the past few hours, and we may need help with that." She paused, glancing back toward the street. "Well, I'll be. Isn't that Chris Marks pulling into his driveway across the way? I guess he's just getting off his shift. We could use someone official to help us."

"It is. I'll go grab him," Sydney said. And off she went.

The rest of them headed into the church.

Several minutes later, with the tea kettle screaming on the stove and half a dozen women pouring over a table strategizing, Sydney jogged down the stairs and into the church basement with Harbor Falls Police Officer Chris Marks in tow.

"I see you ladies are doing some organizing here," he commented.

Six heads jerked up at the sound of his voice.

"Yes, we are," Gracie said. "Can you help us, Chris?"

He nodded. "I can. In fact, I have information." He crowded in between Lucki and Geraldine and then reached for some paper. "May I use that pencil?" He pointed to the short one lying on the table in front of Gracie.

"Of course." She pushed it closer to him.

Chris started drawing on the large preschool-sized writing paper. "Okay," he began. "Here is Harbor Falls, and over there is Dalton Springs. In the middle are two things—the Sweet Hart Inn and Falls Mountain." He drew all the landmarks.

"Don't forget the lake," Lucki told him.

A gasp went up from the women.

Lucki stared. "I don't think she's in the lake! Just making an observation!"

"Well, good Lord. Let's keep that thought out of our heads!"

Chris cleared his throat. "Pretty sure no one is in the lake," he said. "Would be impossible to slide off the road that far."

The group sighed.

Chris continued sketching. "Now, we know Nora took off from Suzie's about six o'clock this evening." He put the point of the pencil on the box that represented Sweet Hart Inn. "Her father was expecting her *here*, at the family farm outside Dalton Springs,"—he made an X for the farm—"at seven o'clock for dinner. Normally, the drive takes about forty minutes. By eight o'clock, Nora still had not shown up."

They all stared at the makeshift map.

"She would have taken this route, right?" Gracie leaned over and traced from Suzie's house, around the lake and through the foothills of the mountain, to end up at the farm.

"It's the only direct route. Yes. If she took the long way, she would have to go through Asheville and backtrack, and that would have taken several hours. No, it's likely she took this route."

"Then we know what road she's on. We just search there."

Chris nodded. "Probably. But there are cars stranded all along the foothills and lake roads, according to police reports, and it will take a while to get through. But there is also more."

"Oh?"

"Yes. We also know that Reverend Peters was on his way home from Dalton Springs at about the same time."

"So, he would have come from the opposite direction."

"More than likely, and is also probably stranded somewhere along the way," Chris told them. "And I also learned that the Dalton Springs police department sent a few men out too, heading toward Harbor Falls. They know to keep an eye out for both."

"Good." Geraldine cleared her throat. "Is there anyone coming from this direction?"

Chris nodded. "About thirty minutes ago, Matt Branson, Brad Matthews, and Sam and Jack Ackerman set off from the Inn. I'd say they will all meet up in the middle within the hour, weather conditions and stalled traffic permitting."

Lucki exhaled and tapped the wooden tabletop. "Good. I feel better. Do you all think Nora and Reverend Peters met in the middle too?"

All the women thought about that, glancing at each other. Sydney grinned.

Lucki added then, "Is there anything actually in the middle other than trees and rocks and country road?"

"Not a damn thing," Geraldine said.

Then Chris smiled. "Except for old man Carter's hunting cabin."

BRAD MATTHEWS STARED AT THE TANGLE OF SNOW-covered automobile parts partially illuminated by the headlights of Matt's Dodge pickup truck. He flashed his light over the car and in its vicinity. Shadows filtered by a snow-ice mist interrupted the beams of the truck lights as Sam and Jack crossed the front of the vehicle and joined him. Matt brought up the rear, heading toward them from the second truck.

Brad squinted at his watch. Quarter to ten.

"Sure looks like Nora's car." He sidled up to the open door of the red Camaro and peeked inside. There was no sign of her or the person who was in the other vehicle.

"Yes. And that SUV looks a lot like Reverend Peters' truck."

Brad looked at Sam, then went back to the small four-wheel-drive vehicle. "You're right. It does." He lifted his gaze and glanced about. "I wonder where in the heck they wandered off to?"

"Can't be far." Matt stepped closer. A two-way radio crackled on his belt. "At least the wind has let up. The snow too. Maybe we can track them."

Jack shook his head. "Maybe, but I doubt it. Even though things have eased up, the earlier blowing snow pretty much covered up any tracks."

Retrieving his Maglite from his belt, Matt flashed it over the trees beyond the cars and over the ground in front of them. "You're right. No tracks. They left here a while ago, and who knows what direction."

"Maybe another car picked them up."

Matt flashed the light up the road toward Harbor Falls. "Hard to tell." He shone the light in the opposite direction. "Nothing there either." His radio crackled again.

"I hear something."

"Just static from my two-way."

Brad shook his head. "No, something else."

All four of the men stood and listened. "I think it's another vehicle," said Jack.

Before long, lights shone around the curve in the Harbor Falls direction and briefly flashed into their eyes. Each of the men stepped backward toward the shoulder. A Harbor Falls Police Department four-wheel-drive vehicle slowly made its way toward the crew. In a flash, all four doors flung open and out came Matt's fellow officer Chris Marks, followed by Mary Lou Nash, Lucki Stevenson, and Gracie Hart. Suzie Matthews exited last.

Brad cleared his throat, stepped toward the newcomers, and looked at his wife. "I thought you were staying home. You and Becca were command central. What happened to that plan?"

SUZIE BRACED HER HANDS ON HER HIPS AND SMILED wickedly at her husband. "You know I don't always do what I'm told, Brad Matthews." If there was one thing that her husband should know by now, it was that she rarely did what was expected.

His gaze narrowed, and he cocked his head disapprovingly, but behind that façade, she knew her unconventional ways still intrigued and amused her husband.

"True. Who is with Petey?"

"Sydney." Suzie shoved her hands into her coat pockets. She nodded toward Chris and the others. "They stopped by the inn before heading out of town. Sydney wasn't feeling well, so I told her to stay in with Petey—who was still asleep, by the way—and that I would come in her place. She's in touch with Becca, so all is good there. Besides, I feel responsible for Nora. I should have made her spend the night."

Matt's radio interrupted, crackly loudly, and he pulled it from his belt, listening. Everyone else paused and listened too. A voice came through barely, and Matt squinted, holding the thing to his ear, while he listened. He punched a button. "Roger that. We're near Carter's Bend, about ten miles out of Dalton Springs."

More crackle and listening. "10-4," Matt said, and looked

back to the crowd. "Poor reception, but Dalton Springs should be here momentarily, with an EMT."

"Good." Brad continued. "More eyes and ears and hands, the better. Let's hope we don't need that EMT." Turning back to Suzie, he said, "Look. Nora made her own decision. There is nothing for you to feel responsible for."

"Well, but there is more."

"More?"

"Of course! When I learned Reverend Peters was also missing, I felt in my heart-of-hearts my help would be needed."

Brad glanced at the men briefly and shook his head. "Your help? In what way?"

Suzie sighed and rolled her eyes. "I smell a potential matchmaking event that may or may not require my support. Either way, I need to be here."

"That's ridiculous."

Suzie shook her head. "Not really. Both Rock and Nora have sought my matchmaking expertise on previous occasions, so I think it's fitting. I may need to be here for moral support, if anything."

Mary Lou squealed and jumped up and down a little, standing behind her.

"No Suzie. This is not the time or place."

She sidled up to her husband, grasped the front of his jacket, reached up on her tiptoes so as to make herself as tall as she could, and whispered to Brad. "Every time and every place are the right time and place for matchmaking, Brad Matthews. Now stand back and let me do my work."

Sam Ackerman snickered on the sidelines. "Don't mess with her when she's determined, man. I can tell you from experience."

"You're talking to the master, here." Brad snorted. "First objective, though, is to find the missing pair."

"Of course." She nodded. "And we will find them soon. I

know it." She glanced to Brad's right. "Is that her car?"

"We think so."

"And Reverend Peters'?" Lucki asked.

"We think so too," Sam echoed.

"Then where are they?"

Brad shrugged. "We don't know."

Suzie stepped back. "We do. At least, we think we know where could be."

"Where?"

Suzie rolled her eyes. "Goodness. I can't believe you haven't figured it out yet. Matt just said it a second ago. We're at Carter's Bend. Hence...."

Brad held up a hand. "Suzie, we just got here ourselves. You're speculating. Besides, we need a plan."

Chris stepped forward. "We already have a plan, Brad. In fact," he glanced about, then pointed his light down the road about twelve feet. "I'd start in the vicinity of that fallen-over mailbox. I'm pretty sure that if we follow that path, we'll find old man Carter's cabin."

"Hell, I nearly forgot about that place," Matt said. "I used to hunt this area years ago."

"You know where it is?"

His head dipped in a nod. "Pretty much, yes."

At that moment, car lights flashed onto the scene from both directions. From the south, the Dalton Springs Police Department arrived. From the north and Harbor Falls came a second SUV. Both vehicles stopped, doors flung open, and the crowd grew.

"There's the rest of the posse," Lucki exclaimed.

"The pick-a-littles," Gracie added.

"Who?"

Suzie grabbed her husband's coat sleeve. "Never mind. Reinforcements." She squared herself, as if taking command of the throng, and then pointed to Matt. "Show us the way."

Chapter Seven

Nora stirred, stretching beneath the quilt. Her body ached in strange places, but she was warm, cocooned by the soft crackle of the fire and the faint scent of pine smoke. When she blinked fully awake, she found Rock crouched by the hearth again, coaxing life into the embers with the poker. He paused the poking momentarily and stared into the flicker. She watched him—he seemed lost in thought—as several seconds ticked by.

His silence evoked a strange emotion, rolling over her like a warm but questionable blanket of comfort.

He's lonely.

Suddenly, a brief snippet of their earlier conversation sailed into her head.

Who is waiting for you to come home?

No one. I live alone.

She spoke before she had time to edit her thoughts. "If you live alone, then would you have spent your Christmas morning alone, anyway? Without friends or family?"

Rock took a moment before twisting away from the hearth, meeting her gaze. His eyes sent forth that same feeling of emotion she'd sensed earlier, with perhaps a bit of added vulnerability.

"Yes, I would have spent it alone, Nora."

"I... It's difficult for me to believe that you don't have someone. You're so kind, and any woman would be...."

She stopped talking. *Darn it, Nora.*

Their gazes danced around each other for a few seconds. Suddenly, she feared she'd crossed into territory she shouldn't have. "I'm sorry. That was prying. And assuming. I should just stop talking."

Rising, he shook his head. "No, it's not prying or assuming." He joined her on the sofa. "I'm the pastor at the Methodist Church in town. I'm pretty much married to my job."

Nora thought about that. "So that means you're not married...to a woman." *Wait, assumptions again.* "Or a man?"

The words were out of her mouth before she realized it. Her eyes flew wide—she could feel them stretch—and she wished she could retract the statement. Her words were not a question, but a clarifying response, and an affirmation that she needed confirmation.

"I mean, that was personal." She paused for a moment, dragging her gaze away from his and staring back again at the fire. "I'm sorry. It's just that ministers are usually married, and both serve the church, and... And I'm making assumptions and being stereotypical and blabbering again. Sorry, it's none of my business."

Rock didn't immediately respond, and the silence in the room between them was almost deafening. Finally, Nora couldn't help but draw back to look at him.

He smiled, and she found she was a bit intrigued by the way the right corner of his mouth shot up in that little grin.

"No, Nora," he said. "I'm not married." Then his face grew serious. "And you are right. It helps if a minister has a partner, but sometimes fate takes other turns. I just happen to still be single."

"Oh."

He paused, and then questioned, "Are you?"

"Married?" Quickly, she shook her head. "Oh no. Not me. I—"

She what? She both chased and then skittered away from men who got too close? Swore herself on and off men like she swore on and off chocolate? And diet sodas? Yet, longed for someone to call her own? "I'm pretty much married to my job too. I mentioned I own a bookstore in Harbor Falls. Nora's Novel Niche. Maybe you've heard of it."

Nice way to skirt the subject, Nora, and change the direction of the conversation. Par for the course, actually.

"Ah, yes. It used to be called something else. Right?"

"Yes. *Books on Main*. It was my mother's store then. She retired, and I took over. I changed the name and the store's focus a bit."

He nodded. "That's right. She catered mostly to local authors and regional titles, if I remember correctly."

"Yes. Poetry, Appalachian lore and history, and the like. The scope of my shop is broader and a bit more contemporary, with a focus on popular fiction and local artists and such."

"I've been meaning to stop in there."

That made her curious. "Really?"

He nodded. "I try to support local businesses when I can. Probably the only reason I haven't been there yet is because I've been reading a lot online lately, oh, and have been trying out audiobooks."

"We have audiobooks! I can hook you up there too." She smiled.

"So, Harbor Falls is your home?"

"Yes, in a way. I grew up out in the country on a small farm, but I went to Harbor Falls elementary and high schools.

I enjoy living in town now. I made the move into town when I took over the store."

"I wonder if we know any of the same people," he said.

"We might. Probably." Suddenly she was feeling awkward. Rock was a nice man and all, and she was feeling some sort of attraction, but they had just met, and this conversation was turning more and more personal and... "Sorry, I grew up in the Baptist church. Not Methodist."

She sat up a little straighter and rubbed her temple. Her head was hurting again.

"I certainly don't hold that against you, Nora." He grinned again.

"I didn't think you would."

"But one day when you are up to debating religion, I can surely hold my own on the subject."

"Oh. Sure." One day? As if in the future? "I'm just mentioning because if I wasn't Baptist, I'd probably be Methodist, and I would have met you before now and that's probably why we haven't really met, seeing that you do audio-books and all and where else would our paths cross?" Nora sighed and closed her eyes. "Babbling again."

"I understood every word—and probably some unspoken."

She glanced about the cabin, avoiding eye contact with him.

"Nora, do I make you nervous?"

Her skittering gaze suddenly halted and landed squarely on his. She gulped and decided to be honest. "Yes. All of a sudden, you do."

The fire crackled loudly as a log shifted inside the fireplace, and the flames licked higher. Rock jerked toward the sound, and Nora watched him, wondering what he was thinking right that minute. Suddenly, the wind rushed against the shuttered windows, shaking them, and sucking the flames higher into the chimney.

He stood and stared into the fire, and Nora felt like a fool. Why had she said that?

ROCK IMMEDIATELY KNEW HE HAD TO CHANGE THE course of events. Turning back toward Nora, he gathered the towel and bowl of melted snow and put some distance between them.

"My apologies," he said. "I didn't mean to make you nervous with my questions. I was simply trying to ease into some conversation and help you relax. But I have made you uncomfortable."

Nora stood as well, reaching out, and touched his hand. "No. Seriously. It's me. No apologies, Reverend Peters."

Reverend Peters. Hadn't she called him Rock earlier? Maybe that was in his head.

"Are you certain?"

She nodded. "I'm positive." She bit her lip and then added. "I—well, I, oh...you don't want to hear about that."

Rock grinned again. He liked the cute way she could flip a conversation. "Maybe I do. I'm a good listener." He paused and watched Nora study his face.

"I guess that's a prerequisite for your job. The listening thing."

"It certainly helps."

She stared a little longer into his eyes. Rock rather liked the vulnerability she seemed to show him right now. Was trust a part of that too?

"I don't have an outstanding track record with relationships," she began. "I mean—and so when I have feelings, I rarely trust myself."

Ah, trust. "Feelings?" He perked up at that statement.

She drew her bottom lip in with her teeth. "I mean, well, yes. I find you attractive and very nice, and it is ridiculous because we are in a crisis here, of sorts, and it is the last thing I should think about, but it makes me wonder if God truly does answer prayers. *Oops.*" Nora slapped her hand over her mouth. "Sorry, I didn't mean to say that out loud."

Rock eyed her. "Of course, God answers prayers, Nora, if it's God's will to do so. What did you pray for?"

Her eyes went wide and round. "I'll leave that to God and me."

There was no doubt this woman warmed his heart. She was sweet and honest, and a chatterbox all rolled into one. And he found her darned near irresistible.

Rock swallowed. "I find you appealing as well, Miss Nora Patterson, and I don't think it's ridiculous."

Her face brightened. "You don't?"

Shaking his head, he replied. "No, I don't."

"Oh."

He stepped closer. "In fact, once we get out of here, maybe you'll let me take you to dinner and we can discuss further. But if you want to talk about that prayer now, I have a little experience in the area. I don't mind."

Nora shook her head. "No. It's not the kind of prayer that is open for discussion. It's sort of a private thing."

She paused, and Rock felt so drawn into her eyes he wanted to step right through them and into her heart. Nora continued, "I mean—" her voice softened, and he moved closer "—after all, I think in time I will know the answer."

Rock felt lost.

And for the briefest moment, his gaze played deeper into her eyes and then danced lower over her lips. An urgent desire to kiss her, to taste her lips, came over him. Perhaps simply a quick nibble, slightly missing her lips but grazing her cheek. Maybe touching the corner of her mouth.

Could he pull that off?

Would it offend her?

Just one little brush of his lips with hers was all he needed, wanted.

For one, to satisfy his own curiosity, not to mention his lips, and two, to quell the growing need inside of him to be closer to her.

But he couldn't do that. Right? It wouldn't be the thing to do. It was against his own personal standards of conduct. A minister didn't go around kissing women he'd rescued just because her eyes mesmerized him so, and because her soft voice played him like a siren's song. No, he couldn't give in to all of that. Could he?

Besides, what would she think? She'd likely run fast and far. That is, if she could.

No. If he ever kissed Nora Patterson, he wanted it to be on fair ground. Being stranded in this cabin was not fair. They were captive here in many respects. No means of escape for either of them, should the situation go from intriguing to uncomfortable.

No. No kissing allowed. Not there.

If Nora ever allowed him the pleasure of a kiss, he wanted to make sure all the conditions surrounding that kiss were perfect.

He stepped away. It was almost painful to do so.

But he was powerless to move very far... and stay away. He simply stood there, staring into her soul, her heart it seemed, her eyes gazing back up into his. It was if some sort of magic was happening between them, holding them both spellbound.

"Christmas magic?" he whispered, surprised the words actually passed from his lips.

"What?" Nora uttered back.

He paused, his gaze dropping to her lips. "Did I say that out loud?" Now who is flipping the conversation?

"You said something about Christmas magic. Do you... believe...?" Her words trailed off, disappearing into the depths of the dreamlike atmosphere around them.

"Right now, I believe in anything." He leaned in, physically unable to keep his distance any longer, to deny his lips from grazing hers, and—

Bang! Bang! Bang!

Shouting. Outside.

"Nora, are you in there! Reverend Peters?"

The cabin door burst open with a flurry of wind, snow, and a bevy of Harbor Falls townsfolk.

Chapter Eight

J ust as Nora's heartbeat kicked up its cadence...

As Rock's lips descended, and she waited for the soft touch of his kiss...

As she felt the blush of heat warm her cheeks and the rush of blood through her capillaries...

Just as everything in her world collided into a single moment of clarity, punctuated with a flash of emotion, and an accelerated sense of awareness...

And just as Rock's gaze peered into hers, pierced her soul, claimed her heart....

The cabin door flew open and banged against the inside wall. People rushed into the cabin. Shouting. Trampling all over everything.

Even her heart.

Especially her heart.

People!

Suzie and Brad. Sam and Jack Ackerman. Then more people. Harbor Falls townsfolk from Rock's church, she quickly assumed, from the way they all rushed inside calling him Reverend. There were police officers from both Harbor Falls and Dalton Springs.

And then the EMTs.

They all flooded the room, and in Nora's brain, everything fast-tracked to high-speed, lickety-split, and interchangeably with slow-motion commotion. So much so that she had difficulty keeping up with everything. Talk and chatter. Questions and exclamations. And more questions.

Her head spun.

She took in bits and snatches of conversation. Everyone, it seemed, was out looking for them with four-wheel-drive trucks with plows, and anything else that could get through the snow. The storm had hit the mountain hard, and more people than Nora and Rock were stranded, she'd learned.

Then she spotted him coming into the cabin. "Dad? Dad!" She jumped up and jogged toward him, ignoring a slight dizzy sensation.

"Sweetheart! I was so worried." Her father's arms folded around her in a bear hug so tight she could barely breathe.

"Oh, Daddy. I'm fine. Rock took good care of me. You shouldn't be out in this weather!"

He clasped her close. "How could I not come? You're all I have."

"Oh, Daddy." She felt the sting of tears.

Pulling back, her father looked into her face, brushing hair out of her eyes. Nora took in the tears rimming his lower lids too.

"You have a bruise up here and some dried blood. We need to get that taken care of."

Nodding, she replied, "We will. Now that you've found us."

He caught her up in another tight hug then, and Nora thought he might never let her go. She could only imagine how worried he'd been. This had not been a good year.

She caught Rock's gaze over her father's shoulder and briefly held it. An EMT was chatting with him and Rock, absentmindedly it seemed, nodded back. She couldn't hear what either of them were saying, but whatever it was, Rock's gaze was still glued to her. The EMT looked like he was checking him over—for injuries, she guessed—but she noticed Rock kept gesturing toward her.

Then she heard him say a little louder. "I am fine. Please check Nora. She took quite a bump on the head and was unconscious for a while."

He was putting her first. Had she ever dated a man who put her first? Well, yes, probably. But his caring and empathy were endearing, and she had to admit that she liked that feeling.

"All right, Reverend." The EMT turned her way.

She took a swaying step backward. Suddenly, she felt icky and weird. Her head pounded as she stood there, her knees feeling as though they could give way, her stomach kind of queasy. Suzie swept closer, saying words she couldn't understand—saying them both to her and to her father. Although it sounded like a mini-lecture about weather and safety, she wasn't certain that it was. Perhaps those words were in Nora's head, maybe in her subconscious. Still, the woman doted on her, coddling and wrapping a warm coat about her shoulders.

Suzie assured her father that they'd get her to the hospital as soon as possible. Her father didn't move far from Nora's side. The Dalton Springs EMT rushed closer.

"Let me check you out, miss," he said. "How are you feeling?"

"Dizzy."

"What's your name?"

"Nora."

"Good." He eyed her then, studying her face, checking her pupils, and examining her temple. While her father hovered,

Nora tolerated the EMT's questions and prodding. Suzie watched her like a hawk.

"Miss Nora," the EMT said to her, "you're going to be just fine, but let's get you up to the road and have you checked out at the hospital. Okay?"

Nora nodded and realized that sudden movement made her head hurt more. "Sure."

"All right then."

She saw the man motion to Suzie and then glance with concern toward her father. Suzie put an arm around Nora's waist and shepherded her toward the cabin door. "Let's just get you the hell out of here and find her some medical care pronto."

The EMT mumbled something too, and suddenly it seemed Suzie was also mumbling. Words. Gibberish. What were they saying?

Nora caught Rock's last peek her way before he, too, was swept away. A swarm of church people shifted him in the opposite direction. Her world felt like it was moving in weird slow motion.

They were taking Rock away from her? No!

She snapped at Suzie. "Stop!" Then seeing Suzie's startled expression, she immediately apologized. "Oh, I'm so sorry. I...."

With her last bit of clarity and effort, she searched the room for Rock's eyes. Couldn't find them. And then, the sound of blood rushing to her head filled her ears, and she started sliding into a dark tunnel.

"Nora!" Suzie's high-pitched scream ripped through the cabin.

Over the din, she heard Rock's deep male voice echo the same. "Nora!"

She hit the floor, only half-aware of what was happening around her and powerless to do much about it.

Suzie fluttered over her, barking orders. Instantly, it seemed, someone lifted and carried her out of the cabin, and up the snowy lane toward the road—the same way she had arrived.

She guessed.

Rock?

It was pitch dark, but there were enough people with flashlights to light the way this time. And thank God, the snow and wind had stopped.

Nora tucked her head into the warm chest of whoever was holding her and closed her eyes. She sniffed for aftershave. Nothing. Her last thought was of Rock, and was he truly about to kiss her earlier, or was it only a figment of her imagination?

"Christmas magic," she mumbled.

"What sweetheart?"

"Are you my Christmas magic?"

The arms of the man carrying her squeezed her tighter and closer. She burrowed in too and found the spicy warmth she sought and the comfort of his arms.

"I hope so," came the soft words back. Her heart swelled.

Her world blurred into a whirl of noise and movement— boots crunching in snow, radios crackling, flashlights bobbing through the dark. Somewhere in that chaos, she caught Rock's voice, deep and steady, giving quiet instructions. The calm in it cut through the confusion like light through fog.

When the EMTs brought the stretcher, he was there, brushing her hair away from her wound, holding her hand while they lifted her into the rig. "I'm right here, Nora," he murmured, the words wrapping around her like the quilt had in the cabin. "You're safe now."

The siren wailed as they started around the mountain, a lonely, echoing sound that made her think of Christmas bells heard from far away. One EMT rode with them, talking to the hospital and checking her vital signs.

Rock rode beside her, one arm braced against the wall for balance, the other hand still holding hers. Every bump in the road made her head throb, but his thumb tracing slow circles against her palm steadied her breathing.

She turned her head slightly, just enough to see him. "You didn't have to—"

"I *did* have to," he interrupted gently. "And I'm not going anywhere until I know you're okay."

The look in his eyes silenced any protest. She closed hers again, letting the rhythm of his breathing soothe her back toward calm, and the rock of the vehicle lull her into a semi-sleep.

The ride to the hospital blurred into fragments—red lights flashing through frosted glass, voices calling numbers she didn't understand, Rock's hand never leaving hers. Somewhere between the whine of the siren and the soft lull of exhaustion, her mind began to drift.

She floated in that quiet space between waking and dreaming, feeling the pull of sleep and the ache behind her eyes. Memories flickered like candlelight: her mother's laughter, the scent of cinnamon from Suzie's kitchen, the way Rock's voice had steadied her when she was scared.

Who was this man who had appeared out of nowhere and held her together when everything else had come undone? A stranger—and yet, not. It was as if her heart recognized something her head hadn't yet caught up to.

Christmas magic, she thought dimly, and a smile ghosted her lips.

In the haze, she felt his thumb trace small circles across her palm, gentle and reassuring. The simple rhythm calmed the storm inside her more than any medicine could. She wanted to tell him thank you, to tell him she wasn't afraid anymore—but the words tangled in her throat.

I prayed for someone this Christmas, she remembered, the thought soft and blurry, *someone who would see me. Maybe I didn't know what I was really asking for until now.*

The siren quieted. The hum of movement surrounded her again—doors opening, voices echoing down bright hallways—but Rock's voice was still the one she heard above the rest. His tone was calm, sure, protective. And in that steady cadence, Nora felt something anchor inside her—a fragile, shining thread of faith and possibility.

By the time they wheeled her inside and the bright lights hit her face, she knew two things for certain: she was alive, and she wasn't alone.

Sleep came in slow waves, tugging her under as warmth replaced fear. Voices faded into whispers; the scent of antiseptic mingled with the faint trace of smoke still clinging to her hair. Somewhere close, she thought she felt Rock's hand squeeze hers one last time before everything went still. When she drifted fully into darkness, it wasn't with dread but with the quiet certainty that she'd been carried through the storm —for a reason.

Chapter Nine

Rock leaned back in the hard plastic chair, exhaustion tugging at him from every direction, but he couldn't bring himself to close his eyes. The rhythmic hum of hospital machines and the slow rise and fall of Nora's breathing were the most beautiful sounds he'd ever heard.

For hours he'd watched over parishioners in hospital rooms—offering prayers, comfort, the usual words a minister was expected to give—but this felt different. There was no distance here, no sense of duty. This was personal. The sight of her, pale against the white sheets yet alive, filled him with something raw and unsteady. Gratitude, yes—but also awe.

He'd always believed faith required surrender, and for the first time he understood what that truly meant. Sitting here, fingers brushing lightly over Nora's hand, he wasn't the shepherd guiding someone else's flock. He was a man, stripped bare of sermons and expectations, humbled by grace he hadn't earned.

"Thank You," he whispered into the stillness. "For her. For tonight. For the chance to feel something real again."

Nora stirred faintly, her lashes fluttering, and he froze—half afraid to move, half desperate to keep watching her. The fluorescent lights painted her hair in soft gold, and he thought of the firelight that had first fallen across her face. Even bruised, she was beautiful.

He caught himself smiling and shook his head. "You've outdone Yourself again, Lord," he murmured with quiet humor. "I can't say I understand the plan, but I think I'm starting to see the outline."

The pulse monitor continued its slow, steady beat, and Rock felt something in his own heart match the rhythm.

He had never in his life been so quickly and utterly smitten with a woman.

As she lay there in the hospital bed, he watched her every movement. An eye flutter. Her lips trembling. A finger twitching.

He glanced toward the window, where snow streaked past the flashing lights outside the hospital, and whispered a silent prayer. *Thank You, Lord. For the cabin. For the fire. For bringing her to me safe.* His throat tightened. *And if there's more You want from this... Show me how to keep her close.*

Nora stirred, squeezing his fingers faintly, and he smiled. Maybe that was answer enough for now.

How had he lived all these years without her?

That seemed a ridiculous notion. Did it not?

But that was how he felt. No other woman had captured his heart so quickly.

Oh, he'd had a semi-serious relationship or two in his three-plus decades of living, but nothing to compare with the immediate and overwhelming spark of attraction and sense of rightness he felt for Nora. Why he had not met her yet, in this small town of Harbor Falls, he did not know—unless, perhaps, the Lord was saving their meeting for the precise time that they would both be ready and receptive to the idea of falling in love.

God has a plan.

And he needed to remember that. Was Nora part of His plan for him, all along?

He trusted that was the case. For many years he had questioned why he'd not been coupled with the woman to share his life, his world. He knew it would have to be the right woman, one who could be with him, love him as he was. He couldn't, wouldn't, change who he was in life for any woman who didn't understand his calling. And he would expect no woman to change for him.

Would Nora accept him? Understand his life's work?

Time would tell, he supposed, and he simply had to keep moving. Keep putting one foot in front of the other and take the steps he needed to take in order to find out.

If, by chance, God had landed Nora in his lap at this moment...

If he had placed her into his life precisely so...

If it were that Christmas magic did exist a little...

Who was he to question a plan that was greater than them both?

Conventional wisdom told him he could not fall in love so quickly, but his heart was ready, and he wanted nothing more than to absorb Nora and everything that went with her into his life. He could only hope she felt the same.

Perhaps that's where the magic of Christmas would lend a hand. He certainly didn't know how any of it would play out, but what he knew was that he would not let this opportunity pass him by.

As he sat beside Nora's bed watching her sleep, her small right hand tucked between his two larger ones, his heart was full and, on some level, he knew the timing was right. That this woman was right. Whatever past either of them had didn't matter—because in the future, they would walk hand in hand, side by side.

He knew that with all his being.

She stirred, and his heart fluttered. Nora moaned softly in her sleep, and he reached to stroke her cheek and comfort her. He prayed that he'd have a thousand and more nights to watch her sleep. To love her and protect her and take care of her when she needed him most.

This night was the first.

This Christmas was their beginning.

<hr />

SOMETIME LATER, NORA BLINKED HERSELF AWAKE and sat alone in her hospital room staring out the window at the cold, blustery morning. She recalled very little of the trip around the mountain to the hospital, but remembered being poked, prodded, examined, bandaged, medicated, and hydrated after she'd arrived.

Merry Christmas to me.

By the time they reached the emergency bay in the night, the snow had slowed to a gentle drift, soft flakes swirling beneath the lights. Somehow, the world felt quiet again—peaceful. Orderlies hurried forward with blankets, their voices crisp and efficient, but all Nora could focus on was Rock's hand slipping from hers as they wheeled her inside. He hesitated only long enough to whisper, "I'll be right behind you," and she believed him.

After that, all she remembered was the doctor saying she could sleep, and in fact, he was ordering a sedative. Good news, no concussion. She had a nasty bump on the head—complete with ugly bruising—which might eventually creep down to her eyebrow, the nurse told her. Her contusions were minor, clean now and dressed with antibacterial ointment.

Her queasiness was likely from not having eaten, even though she'd loaded up on sweets at Suzie's. Hence, her blood sugar level may have been off. Plus, she'd not had fluids for several hours, so she was dehydrated.

Still, she was deemed on the mend, but the doctor suggested she follow up with her doctor as soon as possible.

Yes, everything accounted for and explained, except for the gnawing and escalating emptiness in her chest.

Her heart.

Nora sighed and frowned.

She missed Rock and wondered just how that could be? She barely knew the man.

Maybe she missed the idea of getting to know him better. Maybe that was it.

She was actually happy to have had a little quiet time this morning to think about all that had happened.

This encounter with Rock had shaken her—not physically, but emotionally. Her feelings for him were strong, and she didn't understand how that could happen so quickly. But was all that simply because of the situation they'd been thrust into? There was a syndrome for that, right? When women fall in love with their protectors in a dangerous situation?

Of course, he had rescued her, and she was very grateful. In fact, she wondered how she could ever repay his kindness. But it was impossibly silly to think that she had fallen in love with the man in a few short, tension-filled hours. Right?

Sighing, she closed her eyes. Yes, it was all ridiculously impossible. She'd worked at falling in love for years, and it hadn't happened. Why would she think it could happen so easily and so quickly this time? And when she least expected it?

Maybe that's where she'd gone wrong all those times before.

Maybe things happen when you least expect them.

No matter what she was feeling, she was not in love with Reverend Rock Peters. It was the situation. Right? It was just....

A slight knock rapped on the ajar door, and her shoulders sank. *There goes my thinking time.*

"Yes?"

After a moment's hesitation, she heard footsteps. Rock rounded the corner with a cup of coffee in his hand. Her heart jumped a little.

"You awake?" His smile was broad, but a little hesitant.

"Oh, yes. Hi." Her lips twitched at one corner. Truth be told, she wanted to smile big too. "How are you?"

Rock inched closer. "I think the question is, how are you?"

"I'm fine. Had better days, but I'm good now."

He laughed. "I hear all your tests came back fine."

"Whew." She smiled and nodded. "Last night was a blur. I'm not sure what all happened."

He frowned. "I hope you remember a bit of what happened."

She relaxed a little. "I actually remember quite a lot of the cabin. The end part was the blurry part."

Rock's eyes twinkled. "I think last night was one of those instances where no matter how hard you try to steer the ship, it's going to go in the opposite direction."

She shifted to see him better. "I couldn't steer anything at all. And I lost sight of you."

"I carried you to the road."

"You?"

He grinned. "Yes. You think I'm letting anyone else?"

Her face heated. "Well, thank you. For everything you did. I mean it."

"You're welcome. It was my pleasure."

A long, silent pause fell between them. Finally, Nora spoke again. "Did you make your service last night?"

"No. But we'll make up for it next Christmas."

"Seems like this wasn't the Christmas for either of us, was it?"

Rock grinned and pointed to the side of her bed. "Mind if I sit?"

"Of course not." She patted the blanket.

He set the coffee cup on her nightstand and moved to the bed. In the process of sitting next to her, he took both of Nora's hands into his. A small and deliberate thrill raced through her. "So, this wasn't the Christmas you expected either?"

She searched his eyes. "Not really. Not the one I wished, prayed for... Um. Well, maybe. You see, I—"

"I love when you talk in circles like that."

Nora arched a brow. "What?"

He leaned closer. "I adore you, Nora Patterson. Do you think we could spend more time together?"

"More time? Together?"

"Yes. You and me. Like now. Talking and holding hands. Maybe sharing hopes and dreams."

Nora grinned and nodded. "I'd like that."

"Me too." He paused for a moment, then smiled again, his eyes twinkling. "How about New Year's Eve? I hear it can be quite the celebration."

Nora tilted her head. "Reverend Peters. Are you asking me out on a date?"

"I believe I am, Miss Patterson."

"Then my answer is yes. But let's give it a few days. Okay?"

He squeezed her hands and leaned forward. "I was actually hoping to take you home but remembered my old Bronco is dead on the mountain."

"Well, that is a problem, Reverend."

"Rock."

"Of course." Releasing a pent-up sigh, she added, "I'm glad you came. I know this probably sounds strange, but I missed you."

Rock leaned closer, and his voice lowered. "I missed you too, Nora."

Suddenly, she realized Rock was wearing the same clothing he had on last night. "You haven't been home. Have you?"

He shook his head. "Not since yesterday afternoon, before the snowstorm."

"You stayed here all night?"

He paused before responding. "Nora, after the doctors and nurses left, I didn't leave your side until I ventured out for this really bad cup of coffee." He grinned.

"Really?"

Rock nodded. "Really. And there were others in and out too, of course. Checking on you."

"Dad...? And, Suzie?"

"Suzie left for home after we learned you were okay. I insisted she go to her family for Christmas morning, and I assured her I would call her later. A nurse found an empty room for your dad, and I convinced him to sleep for a while. We just had breakfast together, and I told him to finish his coffee while I headed back up to check on you. And yes, I stayed here all night, holding your hand while you slept. I told your dad I would take care of you."

Nora felt the sting of tears. "Why?" she whispered.

He paused, studying her face, staring into her eyes. "Nora, would you think it strange of me if I said that I always want to hold your hand?"

She had no response other than peering back into the depths of his eyes. Finally, tearing up, she asked again. "Why?"

Glancing at their clasped hands then, Rock waited to respond. After a moment, he began. "I didn't want you to be alone, Nora. Not on Christmas Eve. Or Christmas day. And honestly, I didn't want to be alone either. I wanted to be with you."

Nora beamed, and a couple of tears spilled over her eyelids. Little did he know her crazy friends and family would likely converge on them any second. She also knew that wasn't what he meant. "I'm not alone, Rock. Nor are you. Not this Christmas. We're together."

Rock smiled, brought her hands to his lips, and placed a soft kiss on her knuckles. "If I have anything to say about it, Miss Nora Patterson, you won't be alone this Christmas, or any Christmas to come."

Nora smiled, and her heart soared.

Thank you, God.

Epilogue

This Christmas

Midnight, Christmas Eve, One Year Later....

THE MAN STANDING IN THE VESTIBULE OF THE FIRST Methodist Church of Harbor Falls was not Reverend Rockford Peters.

The new minister's name was Marshall Evans. He had just closed the midnight candlelight service, moved out from behind the pulpit to face the congregation, and quietly asked his parishioners to stay seated for a few moments longer.

"Trust me," he said.

The crowd twittered.

Then Reverend Rockford Peters appeared from a doorway to the right. He approached the new minister and stood on his left, facing his former parishioners.

The organist began playing *The Wedding March.*

The people giddily sighed, stood, and turned. Even though the ceremony was kept a secret, everyone instinctively knew what was happening.

Nora Renee Patterson strolled down the aisle on her father's arm and made her way toward her fiancé. She wore a snowy-white wedding dress with embroidery that actually sparkled. All eyes in the church were on her—and hers were on her future husband.

Her love. Her life. Her rock.

My Rock.

"We are gathered together this Holy night," Reverend Evans began....

Her father wept as he handed over his daughter to Rock, saying, "Her mother and I give her to you, to love and to keep, to cherish and protect."

Nora cried as she held her father, looked deep into his eyes, and turned back to face the man of her dreams. She cried again as Rock placed a gold band on the third finger of her left hand. He shed tears as she placed one on his finger..

"I do."

"I do, too."

"You may kiss your bride, Reverend Peters."

He did. Thoroughly. And the parishioners giggled and cheered.

"To the congregation of the First Methodist Church of Harbor Falls, I present Reverend and Mrs. Rockford Peters."

Nora smiled and said, "Just call me Nora Patterson-Peters."

Rock laughed and hugged her. Those sitting in the first rows likely heard him say, "I love you, Mrs. Patterson-Peters."

"I love you, too," she whispered back, and kissed him again.

Reverend Evans cleared his throat. "There is a small reception in the basement for those who would like to attend. We welcome you to see Nora and Rock off as they fly out early in the morning. Rock is taking a year sabbatical from the church, and Nora is entrusting the management of her bookstore to Becca Ackerman, so that they can explore new opportunities, and possibly discover new ministries together. We wish them all the luck in the world."

The crowd clapped their approval.

"Please join us in a few minutes," Rock said, "as we share our night with you. But first, I want a few moments with my wife."

As the last notes of the organ faded and the congregation's chatter swelled, Rock laced his fingers with Nora's and led her toward the church doors. The sanctuary lights behind them glowed like a halo, spilling gold onto the snow just beginning to fall.

Outside, the night was still. Snow drifted down in lazy spirals, dusting the steps, the evergreen garland, and the shoulders of the man she loved. For a moment, the rest of the world simply disappeared—just her, Rock, and the hush of winter.

Nora tipped her head back, laughing softly as a flake landed on her lashes. "Do you remember the last time it snowed like this?"

Rock smiled, pulling her close. "How could I forget? You nearly ran me off the road."

She chuckled, the sound muffled against his coat. "Maybe I just needed a little... divine intervention."

"Or divine collision," he teased, brushing a kiss against her temple.

They stood like that for a long while, the air crisp, the world hushed around them. The church bells chimed midnight—the echo of the night they'd first met.

Nora looked up at him, her heart swelling. "You know," she whispered, "I used to think Christmas miracles were just stories people told to make the season sparkle. But I was wrong."

Rock traced her cheek with a gloved hand. "You prayed for one."

"And God answered," she said, smiling. "Not this Christmas... the last one."

He laughed softly. "Well, I'm planning to keep answering that prayer for the rest of our lives."

They turned back toward the church, the soft snow swirling around them like a blessing. Once inside, Nora added to Rock's original invite. "We hope you'll join us for a few Christmas goodies in the basement. After all, there is cake and coffee by Suzie Hart, and you definitely don't want to miss that. Merry Christmas, everyone!"

The congregation rose.

Rock Peters led his bride toward their new life.

Together.

Side by side.

Hand in hand.

A Note from Maddie

Friends,

I hope you enjoyed *Not That Christmas.* This story took a surprise turn for me while writing—I hadn't intended for the faith elements to come through so strongly, but I'm very happy with the story! Do you believe in Christmas magic? Or prayerful miracles? While this book is shorter than many of my stories, I think it still packs quite a punch. I hope it touched your heart.

If you enjoyed this read, then please consider sharing with others. One of the best ways to tell others about the book is to leave a review at Goodreads, or at the bookstore where you purchased the book. You can also leave reviews at my website, maddiejamesbooks.com.

Ready for more Falls Mountain? Scroll on to read the first chapter of *Convince My Heart.*

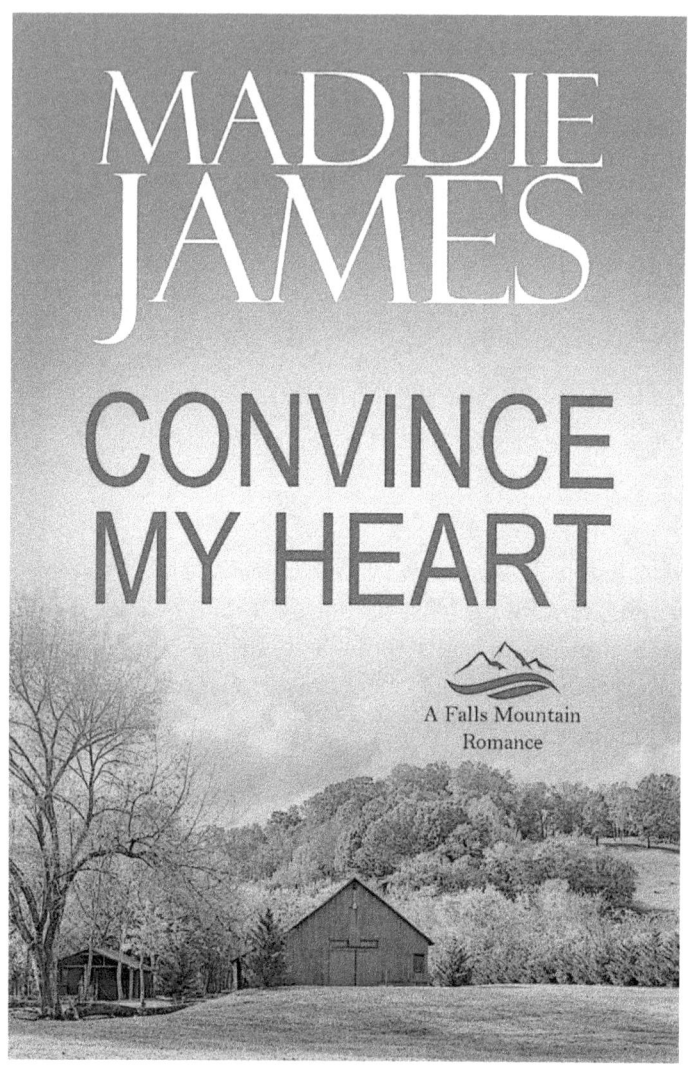

MADDIE JAMES

CONVINCE MY HEART

A Falls Mountain Romance

Convince My Heart
—Chapter One

A woman knows when a man is staring at her. It's a sixth-sense sort of thing. And Samantha Jamieson knew that the man behind her in the grocery checkout line at the Ralph's Grocery Store was staring a hole through her back.

Gulp.

Stifling a sideways glance, she carefully placed her selected items on the counter: a half gallon of milk, a soft drink, a square pack of American cheese slices, three cans of cat food, a box of tampons. A disconnected collection, to be sure, and she still had no clue what was for dinner. She nudged the tampons behind the milk, semi-hiding the box. Only then did her gaze drift to the left, toward *his* groceries.

Interesting.

A large hand placed a divider in front of his order—whipping cream, butter, linguini, Parmesan cheese, fresh mushrooms, a small chicken, and a few items more her brain didn't register—placed one after another onto the moving counter. Much more exciting than her choices. His hands worked back and forth. Large hands, callused hands, with long fingers. The items piled up. Her gaze traveled to his arms, to his chest, throat, face....

Eye contact!

She jerked back to stare at her own purchases. Sadly, they nicely summed up her life. Common. Plain. Boring.

"That will be sixteen-ninety-seven, Sammi," Carly Hartman, the checkout girl, announced. Sammi snapped back to look at the bubble-gum smacking teenager and fumbled in her purse for the money. Handing over a twenty-dollar bill, she kept her eyes riveted straight ahead. Her thoughts, though, were definitely still stuck on the man creating a considerable amount of heated energy beside her.

Stop it, Sammi. You don't ogle men.

Carly thrust her change and receipt forward, popped her gum, and then bagged Sammi's purchases. Risking one more peek to her left, Sammi watched the man take a step toward her. She observed him full-on as he concentrated on his items. His dark brown hair was shaggy, but not quite long enough to reach his collar. His blue jeans were dusty on his tall, lean body. His laced work boots needed a good swipe with a damp rag. She inspected him closer—he was tan, must work outdoors. Dirt showed under his fingernails—farmer? And perspiration stains on his shirt—hmm, maybe construction. He didn't seem the kind of man to buy the ingredients for Chicken Alfredo.

And what kind of man would that be, Sammi? Given your oh-so-limited experience with men? Hmmmm?

But he was handsome. Dirty and sweaty, yes—and likely tired, if the bags under his eyes were any sign—but he was about the best-looking specimen she'd seen around Harbor Falls in quite some time. Must be new in town.

List! Does he have a list?

If so, then there was possible proof of a wife. One who had

sent him to the grocery store for dinner ingredients on his way home from work.

Drat.

Sammi sneaked a closer look and noticed his hands were bare. No list, no ring, not even a thin circle of white where one would have been on that dark, tanned finger. And then she sensed more than knew that he was alone.

Just like her.

Quickly, and a bit startled where her thoughts were taking her, she took the bag of groceries from Carly and left the checkout area. If she ambled along, the man would likely follow her out of the store in a few minutes, and perhaps she could sneak another peek....

No, Sammi.

Only after depositing her bag in the back seat of her Chevrolet sedan did she glance toward the store entrance. On cue, he stepped out. Their gazes clashed again. Sammi's skittered off. Within seconds, she slipped into the driver's seat.

Fumbling in her purse, she groped for her keys and then adjusted her rearview mirror as he stepped in front of her car. Again, their gazes collided, and his skipped off this time. She slipped her key into the ignition of the Chevy.

He kept walking—past the Dodge minivan, an old Jeep Wrangler, the extended-cab pickup truck. He walked until he stopped almost two-thirds of the way down the row at an old flatbed truck.

Sammi twisted the key in her ignition.

Her brain spun. *Farmer, landscaper, construction worker.* One of those.

He put his bag of groceries inside the cab and, in almost the same motion, entered the truck and gunned the engine. The old vehicle rumbled to life—rusty red and peeling, dented fenders, a few old feed sacks tossed on the bed anchored down with a stack of two-by-fours. He pulled out and drove toward her.

Sammi fiddled with her purse again as he passed, then pulled her car out of gear and into drive. Turning the steering wheel and tramping on the accelerator, she fell into place behind him as they both headed out of Ralph's parking lot.

What am I doing? Following a perfect stranger? Why?

"Because I want to know more about a man who looks like that, drives a flatbed pickup, and cooks Chicken Alfredo for Friday night dinner," she mumbled. "Besides, what else do I have to do tonight?"

They approached the intersection, and both turned left. At the next light, Sammi's mystery man sped up and entered the right-hand turn lane. The left lane was the one Sammi needed to go home. A part of her wanted to follow. A part of her wanted to pull up beside him and say something cute like, "Need help with dinner?"

But she settled for the part that made her slow her car, flip on her left blinker, and veer toward the lane that would take her home—home to her quiet little cottage on the edge of town that was perfect for a single, thirty-something spinster. It was the part that went right along with her mousy dishwater-brown hair, her plain but comfortable sneakers, her baggy sweatpants and T-shirt, and her fingernails chewed to the quick.

He hit the accelerator again. Her mystery man turned right on red and headed toward the country.

Sammi followed the line of traffic left and headed for home, thankful for the one bit of excitement at the end of her mundane day. Fully realizing that nothing exciting was ever going to happen to her here in small town of Harbor Falls, unless she took a risk.

Not tonight, Sammi.

The damned phone wouldn't stop ringing.

Caleb Wyatt grimaced and rolled face-first into his pillow. Couldn't a guy get at least one uninterrupted night's sleep around here? Something had disturbed his sleep every night for the past week.

The call couldn't be about Chuck Marshall's mare. He'd delivered that foal this afternoon. He'd taken care of the Henrys' colicky calf the night before that. Tuesday was the night Mrs. Pierson's poodle got intimate with the husky next door. He'd had to calm Mrs. Pierson more than the poodle. And he believed it was Monday when Ryan Campbell's iguana turned yellow, and the child went into hysterics. Seemed his older brother told him he had yellow fever and was going to die.

Of course, the older brother had spray-painted the iguana. And the damn thing might have died if Caleb hadn't gotten the paint off in time.

Was there no peace?

What emergency awaited him tonight?

All this and he hadn't even hung out his veterinarian shingle yet—of course, word traveled fast in small towns. He'd put the ad in the paper only yesterday.

"Hullo?" The receiver barely reached his ear. Caleb glanced at his clock radio. Was it only eleven-fifteen? What early nights he was keeping lately....

"Dr. Wyatt?"

"Mmhmmmm."

"Sorry to bother you, but I saw your advertisement in the Harbor Falls Sun."

"Mmmmm."

"It's an emergency."

He arched a brow. "Oh, umhmmmm?"

"It's my cat."

Caleb opened an eye. The woman sounded anxious. "What, uh..." He cleared his throat, then propped himself up on an elbow. "What seems to be the problem, ma'am?"

"She's... I don't know. She seems to be choking."

"Did she eat something unusual?"

"I don't know!"

"Swallow a coin, a bead, a paper clip?"

"I don't think so."

"Can she breathe?"

"Yes."

"Describe what she's doing."

"Well, actually, she's sort of...gagging, and heaving. Her entire body is trembling. A raspy sound is coming from her throat. And uh, she's spitting up a bit, and making this horrible sound, and...ooh yuck! *There's this slimy gray thing coming out of her throat!*"

"Mrs...." Caleb groaned and burrowed deeper into his pillow.

"Jamieson. Miss."

"Miss Jamieson. Your cat has a hairball."

"A what?"

"A hairball."

"What's that?"

"It's perfectly normal. How long have you had the cat, Miss Jamieson?"

"About a month. She was a stray."

"Have you had her checked out?"

"Uh, no."

Caleb pinched the bridge of his nose. "Bring her by tomorrow. She's in no danger. We'll run the gamut. Shots and so on, and I'll give her something to prevent hairballs. Now if you don't mind, it's late...."

"Of course. Sorry to disturb—"

Caleb barely heard the click of the phone on the other end. His receiver never made it back to the bedside table. He didn't care. There sure were some silly people in the world. This was the first time a damn hairball had interrupted a night's sleep!

———

Sammi assumed she didn't need an appointment. She hoped she'd be able to drop Dicey off at the vet early in the morning, leave so she could run some errands, then pick her up again later in the day. She called the cat Dicey because she was snow white all over, except for two large, perfectly round spots on her back. And the cat had grown so fat over the month she'd had her, that she rolled like dice when she tried to lick her belly.

Sammi hated to admit it, but the cat was growing on her. She was smitten.

She'd kept the cat on a whim, and from the urging of her friend, Emma Jo, to give the big girl a *furever* home, as she'd called it. It was a startling thought at first, being responsible for another living thing, but the idea grew on Sammi.

She had hoped the vet would finish with Dicey by the time she'd finished her errands, so she could go home and relax the rest of the afternoon. After the laundry, of course.

She'd figured wrong.

First, she had a hard time finding the clinic. There was only a small, nondescript ad in the *Harbor Falls Sun* that had given an address. That's where she'd originally found his number. *Dr. Caleb Wyatt,* it read. *Small and Large Animal Practice. 2874 Grimes Mill Road.* Then, the phone number.

There was just one problem.

She was staring at a mailbox that bore the numbers 2874.

The mailbox was rusty and in need of a coat of paint, and it looked as if someone had written the numbers there with a black permanent marker. She knew she was on Grimes Mill Road, about a mile out of town and into the foothills. This had to be it, but where was the clinic? No sign, just a small frame farmhouse and a red barn against the hilly background of trees and mountains. Nothing fancy, and not at all what she'd expected.

The cat mewed in the seat next to her.

"Oh, all right, Dicey. We're here, so let's see what we can find." Sammi pulled off the main road onto the narrow gravel driveway that led to the area between the barn and the house and parked her car.

She tried the house first, knocking on the front door. No answer.

She debated whether to check the barn to find Dr. Caleb Wyatt or just run back into town where she could call a vet who actually had an office.

And she probably would have done that, too, if it hadn't been for the promise she'd made to herself the other day. The day after she'd chickened out, following her dream man out of the grocery store.

Some women wouldn't consider him a dream man, but she couldn't help herself. She'd thought of him often the past two nights. She liked his lanky look and his tanned, weathered appearance. And that he worked outdoors.

He was the total opposite of her. She was short, pale, and worked inside.

That's what made him so interesting.

And well, sexually appealing.

She'd vowed that she was going to spice up her uninteresting life, take some chances and do things a little differently. Take a risk now and then—assert herself.

She would start taking chances.

So, Sammi. Assert yourself.

She looked at the old red barn, swallowed hard, and before she realized it, walked determinedly toward it. She clutched Dicey a little firmer in her arms—she needed to get a carrier—and the plump cat squirmed.

The large wooden door stood ajar. She pushed it fully open, and its hinges squeaked. She poked her head inside.

A large red-coated animal leaped across her line of vision. Sammi bumped into the door, which forced it to open wider. A small squeal ripped from her throat. A dog barked in the corner, then lunged. Something flapped overhead. Feathers and straw swirled in the dusty air. Dicey scratched and clawed, and it was all Sammi could do to hold on to her, those back claws ripping into her shirt sleeves, until the cat wrenched herself from Sammi's arms and went sailing into oblivion.

A chicken squawked.

The cat screeched from somewhere.

The red beast howled in the corner.

Country music blared from... Somewhere.

Sammi breathed in air that smelled like manure.

Standing across the room from her, a man with a dumbfounded expression raised his voice over the cacophony. "Ah, hell. What did you have to go and do that for?"

Balking at his question, Sammi took a deep breath and glanced about. She'd entered a small room at the side of the barn. Bales of straw sat in one corner next to an open stall. She noticed that the red animal bawling was a young calf. The chicken, now quiet, looked down from a rafter. And the dog, a large black Labrador, was panting happily next to its owner.

Where is Dicey?

"I'm... I'm so sorry. I was looking for Dr. Wyatt. Do you know where he is?"

She got a good look at the man then. Shaggy hair, dusty jeans, muscular hands. Mr. Chicken Alfredo himself? Sammi's heart slammed against her chest, and she gulped.

"I'm Caleb Wyatt."

Suddenly, her mouth was drier than an apple fritter-on-a-stick at the state fair. She stammered. "I... I have this cat. I called, and now, well, she's... She jumped out of my arms and she's around here somewhere."

"I don't recall any appointments this morning."

Drat. She knew she should have called. "You said last night. We spoke on the phone—"

Recognition settled in his eyes. "Ah yes. You are the hairball."

Sammi nodded.

"I mean, your cat had a hairball," he corrected. "Somehow I forgot all about it."

"It's okay. I'll just find my cat and come back another time... Make an appointment."

Dr. Wyatt shook his head and glanced off behind the bales of straw. After a moment, he stalked across the room. Sammi watched those long, lean legs as he bent over and snatched Dicey from behind the straw. He held out the cat with a half-smile, and Sammi stepped closer to retrieve the animal.

"Thank you." She gathered Dicey in her arms.

An awkward silence filled the barn room. Dr. Wyatt stared at her. Sammi averted her eyes and gazed at the dirt floor.

"Didn't I see you yesterday at the grocery store?"

Shoot. "Um. Yes. I think."

"I thought so. I'm new in town."

Sammi nodded, averting her gaze. "And I'll come back when it's more convenient," she offered quietly and turned to leave. *So much for taking chances.*

The veterinarian laid a soft hand on her forearm. Sammi

froze and stared at his fingers. "You're here now. There's no reason I can't check your animal. Follow me."

He lifted Dicey from her arms and within seconds, he and her cat were gone, disappearing through another open door. Sammi bit her lip. She had no choice but to follow.

Maybe taking a chance was on her agenda today, after all.

Caleb had immediately recognized the woman. It wasn't her voice, although he now remembered her desperate call from the night before. It was the woman from the grocery store a couple of days ago—the one who had caught his eye. The one who had sporadically and without warning crept into his head intermittently since then.

She'd checked out in front of him. *A half gallon of milk, a soft drink, three cans of cat food, and some other stuff....*

He recalled the timid way she'd glanced at him. How her long, slender fingers had grasped the change from the checkout clerk. The way she had lifted her gaze to look at him with those big, puppy-dog brown eyes as he crossed in front of her Chevy. More than once, her soft and innocent profile had slipped into his mind.

He wouldn't call her a stunning beauty, yet her quiet quality and wholesome good looks attracted him right away. Never drawn to flashy women, he found this woman was anything but—but he certainly liked her looks. Her eyes sparkled, and he wondered if she knew it. Their gazes had skittered off each other a few times in that brief encounter, and it was the one thing that he'd taken with him as they'd parted ways—the innocent and intriguing energy in her eyes.

He'd wondered if he would run into her again. After all, Harbor Falls was a small mountain town where everyone knew everyone else. Or so it had seemed to him. It was one appeal of moving to a close-knit community like Harbor Falls.

The likelihood that he would run into her again was high.

He hadn't expected it to be this morning, though.

Caleb ambled on into the clinic, in the main part of the barn. He knew she strolled along behind him, uncertain, he sensed. She appeared shy and a little timid. They walked through the waiting room and into one of his two examination rooms. Placing a calming hand on the quivering cat's back, he scratched behind the feline's ears. Lifting his gaze to the woman's face, he registered the hesitation in those still twinkling eyes.

The woman held a quiet beauty that had appealed to him days before. And still did now.

"I think she's rid of the hairball," she said tentatively.

Caleb glanced at the cat in his arms. Turning back to his charge, he set the white animal with black spots on the table, leaving a steadying hand on her back. "There, there now, pussycat. You're going to be just fine," he crooned, then glanced up. "Name?"

"Uh, Dicey. Her name is Dicey."

"No, I mean yours."

Her eyes widened. "Oh. Sammi Jamieson."

Caleb extended his free hand. "Caleb Wyatt. Nice to meet you." He offered her a grin. She smiled shyly, then glanced away, but her hand stayed within his for a few seconds longer. Slim, soft fingers lay in his. He took notice of her ragged nails and wondered if she had a habit of biting them. Once again, he sought her eyes, but when she didn't glance up, he quickly dropped her hand and turned to the cat.

"How long did you say you've had her?"

Sammi moved closer to the table and scratched under Dicey's chin. "Oh, about a month. She's a rescue, I guess. She came to my house. I fed her and she stayed. I guess I've given her a *furever* home."

"*Furever*?"

"You know, like *forever* but *furever*, because, well, fur."

He chuckled. "I get it."

"Anyway, I guess I've adopted her."

"Or she's adopted you."

Sammi's eyes met his. "Perhaps."

"Cats usually choose their owners with care." Caleb ran his hands over the animal, giving her a quick once-over, checked her ears for mites, and looked in her mouth. "I'd like to give her all her shots—rabies, feline leukemia, and so on— then check her for worms and such."

"Oh," Sammi answered, "that would be fine."

He picked up the feline and looked into its eyes. "Cats are splendid companions."

"I've never had one before."

"You'll get attached to her pretty quickly."

"I already have."

"Especially if you live alone."

"I know." She paused. "I do."

Caleb waited a moment before setting the cat down, looking into Sammi's face. "You live alone?"

After a moment, Sammi answered, "Yes. I do."

Satisfied he'd gotten the answer he wanted, Caleb turned toward the door leading to the back of the clinic and grinned. This was a switch. He hadn't grinned about a woman in quite some time. He had business to take care of.

He glanced back with what he hoped was a serious look on his face and this time, met her gaze full on. She held it. "If you'll wait here with Dicey, I'll be back in a minute with what I need to finish the examination."

She nodded, and he left.

As he gathered his supplies, Caleb realized he was smiling again. It was a welcome change.

Learn more about *Convince My Heart* on my website, or purchase at your favorite bookstore.

More Harbor Falls & Falls Mountain Books!

Cozy up at the inn where the heart of the Blue Ridge beats strongest...

Welcome to Sweet Hart Inn, a charming bed and breakfast nestled along the peaceful shores of Falls Lake, at the foot of Falls Mountain. At the center of it all is chef and innkeeper Suzie Hart, whose kitchen is always warm, and whose heart is always open. Together with her husband Brad, Suzie serves up matchmaking advice and comfort food, along with second chances, and a generous helping of happily ever after.

The Sweet Hart Inn Books

All of My Heart
Take My Heart
Match My Heart
Tame My Heart
The Dating Game
Miss Matched Hearts
The Husband List
Chase My Heart
No Sweeter Match
One More Kiss

The Falls Mountain Books

Welcome to Falls Mountain, and the quaint town of Harbor Falls.

Tucked deep into the Blue Ridge Mountains, bricked streets, lakeside views, and charming local shops set the scene for small town romance.

In this standalone-but-interconnected series, you'll meet bakers, bookstore owners, chocolatiers, school teachers, and more—all trying to run their businesses, chase their dreams, and keep their hearts in check. But in Harbor Falls, love has a habit of showing up unannounced...

From second chances to secret babies to grumpy-sunshine pairings, each book brings a satisfying happily-ever-after and a cast of characters you'll want to visit again and again.

Falls Mountain Romance is a companion series to the Sweet Hart Inn Romance books by Maddie James.

Dance into My Heart
The Christmas Nanny
The Heartbreaker

Star Crossed
Not This Christmas
Convince My Heart

I hope you'll check out these books, and my other series, on my website at:
www.maddiejamesbooks.com

About Maddie James

Romance with a pulse—small towns, big love, and a dash of drama.

Maddie James writes small-town romance with heart, heat, and the occasional haunting. Her stories range from sweet to spicy, suspenseful to supernatural—happily-ever-afters guaranteed! From stand-alone love stories to binge-worthy series, Maddie delivers love next door, some cowboy kisses, an occasional hint of danger, and just enough drama to keep things interesting.

Get all the drama delivered to your inbox when you sign-on to Maddie's VIP reader list!

Free books, sneak peaks, bonus content, giveaways, and more...

Learn more: maddiejamesbooks.com/pages/newsletter

www.ingramcontent.com/pod-product-compliance
Lightning Source LLC
Chambersburg PA
CBHW072032170626
46811CB00008B/3044